The highwayman pulled Lucinda toward him, plunging his calloused hands inside her cloak. Already she could feel his hot, sour breath on her face. Frantic, she tried to jerk away, but he retained a firm grip on her dress, ripping the flimsy muslin bodice as he flung her roughly to the ground.

Lucinda gathered up all her courage and strength. Wildly lashing out with her walking boot, she kicked him hard on the shin while screaming at the top of her voice, "Help, help!" Her desperate cry died away in the still evening air. There was no one, it seemed, on this deserted country lane to hear or care about the plight of the Lady Lucinda Verney.

Suddenly, there was the sound of a horse galloping and a horseman thundered down on the two ruffians. With a blood-curdling cry, he drew his sword stick and smashed it into the face of one of the rogues. Then he made his horse rear and kicked the other rogue hard in the chest.

Lucinda scrambled to her feet to thank her rescuer. For a brief moment, the moon appeared from the clouds, illuminating the stranger's face. Lucinda's sense of relief turned instantly to horror. The man was wearing a mask! Had she been rescued from one set of criminals to find herself in the hands of another?

Novels by Caroline Courtney

Duchess in Disguise
A Wager For Love
Love Unmasked

Published By
WARNER BOOKS

CAROLINE COURTNEY

Love Unmasked

WARNER BOOKS

A Warner Communications Company

WARNER BOOKS EDITION

Copyright © 1979 by Caroline Courtney
All rights reserved

ISBN 0-446-94054-2

Cover art by Walter Popp

Warner Books, Inc., 75 Rockefeller Plaza, New York, N.Y. 10019

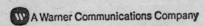 A Warner Communications Company

Printed in the United States of America

First Printing: October, 1979

10 9 8 7 6 5 4 3 2 1

Love Unmasked

ONE

"No! *No!* Release me! I beg you—"

Lucinda's piercing scream of terror was abruptly muffled as the bigger of her two attackers clamped a grimy hand across her mouth. She struggled frantically as they dragged her across the road into a gap in the hawthorn hedge.

"Hold still, you minx!" ordered the second rogue, his eyes glittering cruelly in the gathering darkness. "Now, let's see what pretty trinkets you have to offer me."

Lucinda's heart pounded with fear as she felt his rough hands wrench aside her cloak and finger the soft white skin of her unadorned throat. She winced with pain as he seized her wrists, bruising them in his feverish search for valuable rings and bracelets.

"Nothing!" he spat, flinging her hands down in disgust. "I'll be dashed if I can find so much as a silver pin on the girl."

Lucinda sent up a prayer of thanks that all the Verney family plate and jewelry was at this very moment being cleaned, ready for the arrival tomorrow of her brother Frederick and his bride of three months.

She squirmed violently as the big rogue whirled her round to face him. Although she could not see his expression in the gloom of the March night, nevertheless, she could sense his fury and frustration.

Frightened though she was, Lucinda remained a girl of great courage and spirit. Tossing back her golden curls, she said boldly:

"Release me this instant, you scoundrel! As you see, I have no money or jewels on my person. And I assure you, when my father, the Earl of Waverley, comes to hear about this—"

"Hold your tongue!" shouted the ruffian, gripping her tightly by the shoulders.

He went on, his voice laced with malice, "I'm not partial to having my time wasted. As you have no jewels to offer me, my *pretty* lady, I've a mind to steal something far more valuable instead!"

He pulled Lucinda toward him, plunging his calloused hands inside her cloak. Already, she could feel his hot, sour breath on her face. Frantic, she tried to jerk away, but he retained a firm grip on her dress, ripping the flimsy muslin bodice as he flung her roughly to the ground.

The other rogue laughed coarsely. "Go on. Give the bitch what she deserves. Then I'll have my turn!"

The man knelt over her, his breath coming in short, rapid pants as he clawed the top of her skirt.

Lucinda gathered up all her courage and strength. Wildly lashing out with her walking boot, she kicked him hard on the shin while screaming at the top of her voice, "Help! *Help!*" Her desperate cry died away in the still evening air. There was no one, it seemed, in this deserted country lane to hear or care about the plight of the Lady Lucinda Verney.

Thoroughly maddened by Lucinda's kick, the man muttered grimly to his companion, "Hold her down. I've a mind to tame this wildcat . . . and at the same time teach her a lesson she'll never forget."

Lucinda opened her mouth to scream again, but a hand was pressed roughly across her lips. Tears of despair stung her eyes as she was pinned to the ground and hands began to tear at her dress. She was trapped! There was no escape now from a fate worse than death.

But, as if by a miracle, came the welcome sound of a horse, galloping fast toward them. Cursing, the two blackguards released Lucinda and rushed into the middle of the road.

Looking up, hardly able to believe her eyes, Lucinda saw the silhouette of a large man on horseback thundering down on the two ruffians. The man wasted no time. With a blood-curdling cry, he drew his swordstick and smashed it into the face of one of the rogues.

A high-pitched screech of pain followed as the blood from his broken nose streamed down the man's chin. Lucinda's rescuer paid him no further heed. Jerking his bridle, he made his horse rear and kicked the other rogue hard in the chest. Winded, the scoundrel reeled back, gasping for breath.

The mysterious stranger raised his sword-stick again, but Lucinda's attackers were in no mind to wait for more punishment. Muttering a stream of vicious oaths, they dived through the gap in the hedge and stumbled off across the fields, to disappear fast into the night.

Lucinda scrambled to her feet, holding her cloak tightly around her to hide her torn dress. She felt shaken, but unafraid in the presence of her gallant rescuer.

He laid a gentle hand on her shoulder. "I heard you cry out. Are you hurt?" His deep, cultured voice sounded strangely muffled.

Lucinda shook her golden curls. "I am unhurt. But if you had not arrived when you did . . . I dread to think what would have happened. How can I ever thank you?"

"You should not venture out after dark by yourself," he admonished her gravely.

"I know," replied Lucinda, biting her lip. "I had taken some nourishing brawn to one of the farmers' wives . . . she had just been delivered of her sixth child. I fear I mistook the time."

And Papa would be furious with her when

she reached home! How many times had he told her never to walk abroad alone after dusk. The countryside was teeming with desperate rogues. Penniless, unscrupulous men who terrorized travellers and would stop at nothing if they glimpsed so much as the flash of gold beneath a lady's cloak.

However, reflected Lucinda, now beginning to recover from her ordeal, this time I have been fortunate. Thanks to my noble rescuer. His gloved hand still rested lightly on her shoulder. Although she had no notion as to who he could be, she felt immeasurably reassured by his presence.

For a brief moment, the moon appeared from the clouds, illuminating the stranger's face. Lucinda's sense of relief turned instantly to horror. The man was wearing a mask!

At least—no—it was not a mask, but a black cravat, tied to cover the lower part of his face. Only this one, tantalizing glimpse was allowed her before the capricious moon vanished and the gloom enveloped them once more.

Lucinda shrank back against the hawthorn hedge. The prickles dug mercilessly into her back, but she was oblivious of their vicious stabs. The pain in her back was nothing compared to the icy hand of fear that gripped her as she stared up at the man on the horse. So he was not a gentleman, after all. Unwittingly, she had fallen into the clutches of yet another scoundrel!

"Where do you live?" he enquired.

Now Lucinda had seen his mask, she un-

derstood why his voice had sounded so muffled.

She thought quickly, aware that only a
cool head and quick wits would save her now.
She dared not admit that she lived at Waverley
Hall, under the roof of her father, the Earl.
This man was not a common ruffian like her
two attackers. He belonged to a different, in-
finitely more dangerous breed . . . that of the
gentleman adventurer. He was intelligent, dashing, and obviously completely fearless. Why,
the well-mannered rogue would probably find it
great sport to follow her back to the Hall,
wait until midnight, and then make off with the
celebrated Verney family plate!

With an effort of will, Lucinda kept her
voice steady. "The house down there, at the end
of the lane," she said, indicating the twinkling
lights of the residence owned by the burly
local physician. If this gentleman of the road
attempted to break in there, he would be in
for a shock, reflected Lucinda. The good Dr.
Webster owned few valuables, and it was common knowledge that he always slept with a pistol beneath his pillow.

"Then let us carry you home with all good
speed!" declared the man on the horse. Before
Lucinda could protest, he had reached down
and lifted her onto the saddle in front of him.

His strong arms held her firmly as they cantered down a deserted road filled with the fra-
grant scents of the spring night. Lucinda was
sure he must hear the frantic thudding of her
heart. Was he really taking her to the place she
had said was her home? Or was he about to

carry her off and abduct her? Perhaps he had a mind to hold her hostage, while he ransacked poor Dr. Webster's house.

Lucinda paled at the thought. Imagine the scandal! Papa would never, ever forgive her.

And yet, with the soft evening air blowing through her hair, Lucinda realized to her astonishment that she no longer felt afraid. Why, she could not tell. She was in a most perilous situation, yet she could not stem the amazing sense of elation that was sweeping over her.

Whatever is the matter with me, she wondered, her lovely amethyst-colored eyes sparkling with excitement. I'm being carried through the night in the arms of an adventurer . . . the most dreadful things could be about to happen . . . and yet, somehow, I feel so safe with this man. I *trust* him.

Her sense of security increased as he reined in the horse outside Dr. Webster's house.

"You see, you had no reason to feel afraid," he murmured. "I have brought you safely home."

She twisted in the saddle, trying in the darkness to etch some memory of his face on her mind. But she could see so little, except for the amused gleam of his eyes.

"Who are you?" she whispered.

He laughed. "You could call me a man of the night. And a friend," he said.

His hands tightened around her tiny waist, and she realized he was about to lift her down from the horse. Desperately, she wrenched at the silk cravat tied around his face.

"Oh, no, you don't," he laughed.

He was too swift for her. In one effortless movement he swung her clear of the horse and lightly onto the ground. He himself made no move to dismount.

Lucinda stared up at the commanding figure on the horse. "Thank you for rescuing me. I am most grateful . . . whoever you are."

There was a smile in his voice as he replied, "It is more intriguing, think you not, for us to remain strangers to one another. To me you will always be the beautiful golden-haired girl I was able to rescue from distress. And you must simply remember me as the man from the night . . . and your friend."

With that he bent and took her hand. With exquisite tenderness, he lifted it under his silk scarf and pressed it to his lips.

At his touch, a tremor ran through Lucinda. She closed her eyes, fearful that she would swoon. She was trembling from top to toe. When at last she regained her composure and opened her eyes, the man had gone. Her adventure was over.

All that remained was the receding sound of a horse's hooves echoing through the scented violet night . . . and the burning memory of a stranger's lips kissing her hand.

"Lucinda! Wherever have you been?" Lucinda's brother Robert came dashing to greet her as she slipped into Waverley Hall by the garden door.

Lucinda hugged her cloak tightly round her to conceal her torn bodice and said evasively, "Oh, dear. Has Papa been looking for me?"

"No," grinned Robert, pushing back a wayward strand of his fair hair. "Papa has beat a retreat to the library. Poor Mama is in such a pother over the preparations for Frederick's visit that Papa declared one would have imagined it was the Prince Regent himself who was coming, instead of her very own son. So he's escaped to the library to drink his port in peace."

Lucinda smiled. "No doubt Mama has been asking for me?"

"She wishes to discuss the menus with you," said Robert, "and whether Frederick's wife will regard the damask hangings in her dressing room as too old-fashioned for words. Everything, of course, has to be quite perfect."

Lucinda gave Robert a sympathetic glance. At seventeen, Robert was two years younger than herself, and had just finished his schooling at Eton. She knew he was not looking forward to Frederick's visit. He was only too well aware that one of the topics under discussion between Frederick and Lord Waverley would be the thorny topic of Robert's future.

Robert was the kind of person, Lucinda mused, who loved to be the first to do everything. She remembered that as a child, although he was younger than herself, he had been determined to learn to ride before her. He had been the youngest boy ever to ride with the county hunt ... the first of his set of friends to bag a brace of grouse, and to score a century at cricket. So it had gone on. Whatever the current fashion or interest, Robert was always the leader. And now he had left Eton, he was desperate to be the first of his year to take a commission in the Army, and join the Duke of Wellington's troops in the war against the French.

Lord Waverley, however, had other plans for his younger son. He desired that Robert should stay in Surrey and learn to manage the vast Waverley estates. To this end, Lord Waverley would doubtless have an ally in his heir, for Frederick was a dutiful son who always made a point of agreeing with everything his father said.

Lucinda noticed the despondent droop of Robert's shoulders as they walked up the broad main staircase of the Hall. She felt sorry for her brother, for she knew that, like herself, he craved excitement and adventure. He would find it dull beyond words to incarcerate himself at Waverley when there was in Europe a war waiting to be fought.

At the same time, she knew she would feel hopelessly bereft if Robert left home. They had always been close, and had shared many childhood escapades.

Pausing outside her bedchamber, Lucinda touched her brother on the arm. "Do not fret too much about Frederick's visit," she advised. "It may be that his marriage to Melanie will have given him a broader outlook on life. He may now be prepared to lend his support to the notion of your joining the Army."

A grin suddenly illuminated Robert's boyish face. "Well, I'll certainly give him something to stare at when he arrives tomorrow. Are the you-know-what's ready, sister?"

"I'll finish them off tonight," whispered Lucinda conspiratorially. "But are you sure you know what you are about, Robert? Papa will go up in a cloud of blue smoke when he sets eyes on you tomorrow."

Robert shrugged. "I must take my chances on that. I cannot pass up the opportunity to be first with a new fashion, Lucinda. You know my nature."

"Only too well," laughed his sister. "On your own head be it, then. Now I must tidy myself, and go and calm Mama."

When she had changed her dress and brushed her hair into a halo of golden curls around her lovely face, Lucinda hurried down to the elegant main drawing room. She found her mother sitting on a sofa by the fire. The polished surface of the kidney-shaped table beside her was piled high with menus, scrawled in Lady Waverley's extravagant hand.

"Oh, there you are, Lucinda," exclaimed Lady Waverley, looking thoroughly harassed. "Now tell me. Do you think Frederick will regard oyster sauce with the wild duck as far too common? Should I ask cook to prepare a more unusual, more exotic sauce instead?"

Lucinda drew up a velvet stool and said soothingly, "I am convinced the oyster sauce will do very well, Mama. Besides, as a bridegroom of only three months, I have no doubt that my brother will be too occupied admiring his lovely new wife Melanie than bothering to criticize your table."

Lady Waverley sighed. "But you mind how fussy Frederick is about everything, dear! He is cast in just the same mold as your papa. Oh!" She clapped a ringed hand to her head. "I forgot to tell Cook about the tea!"

"What about it?" asked Lucinda, opening her rosewood workbox and taking out her embroidery.

"Your father complained that the breakfast tea tasted musty. He insists that Cook has been mixing in dried blackberry leaves and stealing the real tea for herself."

"Nonsense!" Lucinda laughed. "The tea tasted perfectly good to me at breakfast. You know Papa tends to have strange fancies. By tomorrow he will have forgotten about the tea, and be insisting instead that his bacon wasn't cured properly."

Lady Waverley murmured, "Really, Lucinda, you must learn to have more respect for your father!" But there was a twinkle in her eyes which belied the severity of her tone. She went on, "I only hope that Melanie will not find us too quaint. After all, we met her only a few times before her wedding to Frederick, and now they live in such style on Curzon Street. After fashionable London, she is bound to find our country ways somewhat rustic."

Lucinda threaded a length of scarlet silk into her needle and commented, "I doubt very much if Melanie is engaged in a bustling social whirl. As you said yourself, Mama, Frederick is so much like Papa. If he really is following in Papa's footsteps, I don't imagine that he and Melanie will have been to more than one ball or assembly since their marriage."

"I must confess, Lucinda," said Lady Waverley, lowering her voice, "your father sometimes puts me in mind of a badger. He just desires to sit at home and see no one and go nowhere. I wouldn't mind for myself, but I do worry about you."

"But I am perfectly happy, Mama!"

Lady Waverley shook her head. "But how are we ever to get you married, Lucinda? Stuck out here in the country, it is impossible for me to introduce you to any eligible young men. We have no near neighbors, apart from Lady Falconbridge, and you know how difficult your father is about allowing us to visit her."

Lucinda's pretty face lit up with amusement. Lady Falconbridge's house was copiously adorned with fashionable colonnades and sculptures. "Pretentious rubbish," Lord Waverly had asserted. "That type of architecture may look magnificent under an azure Greek sky, illuminated by a dazzling white light, but set it under a typical English drizzle and it looks ludicrous. I will not set foot in such an establishment, and neither will any member of my family."

So that had been that. They had returned to the solid lines and mellow red brick of Waverley Hall. From here, Lord Waverley steadfastly refused to emerge, apart from his annual visit to London when Frederick gave an account of his handling of the family stocks and shares.

Lady Waverley took a comfit from the silver dish beside her. "It was such a pity your London season had to be curtailed, Lucinda. I had great hopes for you there."

Lucinda and her parents had gone to stay with Frederick in Curzon Street for her season, but she had barely been presented at Court, and attended one ball, before her father was taken ill, and the family had returned to Surrey. Lord Waverley took a full month to recover, and blamed the London food for his illness, declaring that he was tainted by the smoky atmosphere. "Country air is best," he proclaimed firmly, and he would not hear of Lucinda or her mother visiting London again.

"Now, Mama," Lucinda said, smiling, "you have enough on your mind at present making all the arrangements for Frederick's visit without fretting about my marriage prospects as well."

A frown still creased Lady Waverley's brow. "But I am extremely concerned about you, my dear. After all, you are nineteen, and time is passing. Your father, you must admit, has been most lenient with you up to now. I confess I was most surprised when he allowed you to reject not one, but *two* highly eligible suitors for your hand."

Although her London season had been so short, Lucinda had proved to be an astounding success. Yet her beautiful amethyst eyes widened as she exclaimed, "Oh but, Mama, reflect . . . Sir William Macey was no more than a drooling idiot, while the Duke of Davenport was nearly fifty! I would rather die an old maid than marry either of them."

Lady Waverley did not tell Lucinda that there had, in fact, been a third suitor. But he had fallen at the first post, as he did not possess a title. It was, of course, unthinkable that the daughter of the Earl of Waverley should marry an ordinary man. Instead, she said mildly, "Well, you were fortunate that your father indulged your girlish fancies over those two suitors. But I warn you that next time, he will most like be more severe with you."

Lucinda laughed. "But how is there to be a next time, when I am not allowed to meet any young men?"

"I do not know," confessed her mother, "but I have a notion that your father has something in mind. I spoke to him only this morning about this question of your marriage, and he told me not to fuss, because he would arrange the matter."

Lucinda said lightly, "In that case, I suggest we take heed of my father's advice and trouble ourselves no more with the subject." She affected a yawn. "Now, dearest Mama, if you will excuse me, I would like to retire early tonight."

Lady Waverley smiled. "Of course, you must be fatigued by all the excitement of Frederick's visit. Good night, then, my dear."

Lucinda bent to kiss her. "I will say good night to Papa on my way upstairs," she promised.

The library was one of Lucinda's favorite rooms. She loved its air of peace, and the smell of leather-bound books, the beeswax polish on the mahogany tables, and the apple logs crackling in the huge fireplace.

She found her father sitting in front of the hearth, with his bare feet immersed in a bowl of steaming water. As she bent to kiss him on the forehead, Lucinda saw to her surprise that behind each ear he had placed what looked like roasted turnip parings.

"Good evening, Papa," she murmured, long experience of her father's eccentricities warning her to proceed with caution. "Er . . . are you soaking your tired feet in a mustard bath?"

He glared up at her from beneath his bushy eyebrows. "Not mustard. *Bran,*" he declared.

Lucinda nodded, totally nonplussed. She had never before heard of anyone desiring to sit with his feet in a bowl of watered bran, but then her father had ever been a man of unusual tastes. She said carefully, "Papa, I do not wish to appear inquisitive, or stupid, but why have you placed turnip parings behind your ears?"

Lord Waverley heaved a great sigh. "I should have thought it was obvious. I have a *toothache.*"

Lucinda bit back a shout of laughter. "Oh, yes . . . of course . . . toothache," she said faintly. "How silly of me. But . . . er . . . would you not find it more soothing if I fetched you some warmed oil of cloves for your tooth?"

"You know I don't believe in these new-fangled remedies, daughter." He let out a bellow of laughter. "Ha . . . ha! Do you get it,

Lucinda? New *fang*-led! No, what was good enough for my father is good enough for me. He always cured his toothache with bran water and turnip parings."

"If the tooth is very bad, Papa, you could always have it removed by a tooth-drawer."

"A tooth-drawer?" snorted Lord Waverley. "Have you quite taken leave of your senses, Lucinda? Heavens above, my ancestors go back to William the Conqueror. Do you imagine I would consort with such a common breed of men as *tooth-drawers?*"

"I had just thought . . . to alleviate the pain," murmured Lucinda, pouring out a fresh glass of port for her father.

"I'd rather endure the rack than go near one of those fellows," asserted Lord Waverley. "Why, I heard of one who had his dead wife embalmed and then kept her in a glass case in his drawing room."

Lucinda realized that if she stayed in the library another moment she would dissolve into a fit of unseemly, hysterical giggles. Quickly, she said good night to her father, wished him better, and made her way up to her chamber.

Tucked underneath her pillow was a novel, *Midnight Weddings* by Mrs. Mary Meake, one of Lucinda's favorite authors. Lucinda was a voracious reader of stories of adventure and romance, though she knew that if her father ever discovered her reading such novels, he would burn the books and confine her to her room with only bread and water for a week. Normally, Lucinda read for a while before blowing out her candle, but this night she had some important sewing to finish for her brother Robert.

She slipped into her nightrobe and took the candle across to the windowseat, there to complete her sewing. A March wind had come up and blown the clouds from the sky, so the lawns below her window were silvered with moonlight.

As she sewed her fine, neat stitches, Lucinda pondered on her conversation that evening with her mother. What had she meant, about her father's arranging matters for her marriage? What—or rather, *whom*—had her father in mind? It was true that Papa had been uncommonly indulgent in allowing her to reject two suitors. In Papa's terms, the two beaux had been highly suitable candidates for her hand. Indeed, Lucinda could think of many girls who would have jumped at the opportunity of becoming Lady Macey or the Duchess of Davenport.

But such a sensible, suitable marriage was not what Lucinda wanted. She sighed as she gazed out at the windswept trees of Waverley Park.

"What is the matter with me?" she whispered. "Why am I possessed of such a restless spirit? I love my family dearly. But Papa is such a traditionalist. . . . Sometimes I feel like a butterfly trapped in a silken, loving net. What is it . . . or who is it that I want?"

As she spoke, a solitary cloud scudded across the moon, like a lonely rider in the sky. Lucinda's heart seemed to miss a beat. Her blood raced as she remembered a ride through the scented night, with strong arms around her and a soft breeze blowing through her hair. Once again, she felt carried away on a tide of elation, conscious only of a heady sense of freedom and joy.

No man had ever stirred her like that before. "Oh!" she breathed, her eyes luminous as she gazed out into the moonlight. "Where are you now, my man of the night . . . my friend? Will you ever return to set my shackled spirit free again? Wherever you are, my mysterious stranger, my gallant rescuer, you must know that I am thinking of you."

Softly, she opened the window and blew out a kiss into the enchanted, silvery night . . . toward a man whose name she did not know but who, nevertheless, had captured her heart.

TWO

"They are coming!" cried Lucinda excitedly, waving from an upstairs window as Frederick's magnificent coach advanced at a stately pace up the long front drive of Waverley Hall.

Robert dashed to join his sister at the window. "Oh," he groaned, "look how slowly they are travelling. How typical of Frederick to order his driver to journey at no more than six miles an hour. Why, the newer coaches can cover nine miles in an hour! Frederick could travel here from London in a mere five hours, instead of taking all day over it."

Lucinda was in high spirits at the notion of entertaining visitors. "Frederick was always something of a slow coach, you know, Robert."

Her brother winced. "Really Lucinda,

what a dreadful joke. It's worse than those our father tells, and they are bad enough." His blue eyes widened as he gazed from the window. "Oh, mercy, look what's happened now!"

The coach had drawn up outside the front entrance to the Hall, and three of Lord Waverley's footmen were scurrying forward to assist Melanie from the carriage and attend to the luggage. Ever a staunch upholder of tradition, Lord Waverley still insisted that his footmen wear curled wigs. But today the March wind was in an especially playful mood. . . .

"Poor Gilbert has lost his wig!" laughed Lucinda. "Oh, dear, I do hope Papa has not witnessed that. You know how he loathes unseemly scenes on the front doorstep."

"I must go and change," murmured Robert. "I will join you in the drawing room."

"I hope you know what you are about," whispered Lucinda. "Just so long as you are prepared for fireworks when the family sets eyes on your attire." Then, cupping her hands, she called out to the bewildered footman, "Gilbert! Your wig has blown into the laurel bush. Hurry and you will catch it!"

The distraught footman hurried off in pursuit of his wig. The scramble evoked a disapproving raised eyebrow from Frederick, Viscount Alford and Lord Waverly's, as he slowly descended from his coach. He was a tall, well-built young man with the fair Verney hair and brilliant blue eyes. Although only in his early twenties, Frederick liked to affect a ponderous expression which he imagined lent him an air of authority—but which inevitably reduced Lucinda to giggles.

Gilbert, with the offending wig safely perched upon his domed head, was helping Frederick's wife from the coach. Lucinda had met the Lady Melanie only a few times and so had been unable to form a real impression of her new sister's character, but she certainly seemed a pleasant enough girl. She was of medium height, with dark curly hair and brown eyes as soft as pansies.

I only hope, mused Lucinda, that Melanie has enough backbone to stand up to Frederick. The last thing he needs is a simpering wife who would not say boo to a goose. Or worse, who would not even recognize a goose if it stretched up and bit her on the arm.

The party was now making its way inside, and Lucinda realized that she must hurry to be downstairs in the drawing room in time to greet her brother.

As she entered the drawing room, Lady Waverley drew her aside. "Lucinda, how many times has your father told you that it is most unseemly for young ladies to shout out of windows as you did just now?"

"But, Mama," said Lucinda reasonably, "poor Gilbert had lost his wig. Papa would have been in even more of a quake if he'd seen one of his footmen appearing bareheaded."

Lady Waverley, still inwardly debating the wisdom of the forthcoming duck and oyster sauce, looked totally confused at Lucinda's explanation. Fortunately, at that moment Viscount and Lady Alford were announced, and there were hugs, kisses, and laughter as the family were reunited. When at last they were all seated comfortably before the fire, a servant brought in wine and sugared biscuits.

Frederick smiled at Lucinda. "I am glad to see you in such good health, sister. In fact, I would go so far as to say you look positively dazzling."

"That's enough of that, Frederick," interposed Lord Waverley gruffly. "No cause to go turning the girl's head. Melanie, my dear, I hope you do not allow your servants to burn sea coal in your London house. The smoke taints the food something terrible, you know."

While Melanie murmured words of reassurance to Lord Waverley, Frederick caught his sister's eye and winked. Lucinda smiled across at him. Dear Frederick. Admittedly, he could be somewhat pompous at times. But she could not forget that as children, Frederick had frequently come to her aid when she found herself in one scrape or another, and protected her from their father's short-lived wrath.

With Robert, Frederick's relations had not been so amiable. There had always been rivalry between the two brothers. Frederick, of course, had a head start, being the elder and the heir. But Robert had the advantage of quick wits and an engaging nature. In all, when the two brothers fell into verbal combat, there was very little to choose between them.

It was just as Lady Waverley was explaining that Lady Falconbridge would be joining the men at the hunt tomorrow that Robert chose to make his entrance. Lady Waverley clutched at her pearls, her voice fading away. The whole family sat in stunned silence, staring at Robert as he strolled across the carpet toward them.

Lord Waverley recovered first. "Just *what*," he demanded, in a stentorian voice, "do you think you've got on?"

"Cossak trowsers, sir," said Robert, in a most civil tone of voice. He strode to the middle of the room, bowed to the ladies, then executed a neat turn, revealing the flowing cut of the trowsers, which were gathered at the waist and ankles.

Lord Waverley stared at his own impeccably correct breeches and then at the voluminous garment adorning his younger son. Slowly, his face turned dark purple. "How dare you wear such ridiculous attire in my house . . . in front of your mother . . . your unmarried sister! What damned impudence!"

"But, sir, it is a style set by the Czar of Russia. Why, everyone in London is cutting a dash in these new trowsers."

The family looked expectantly at Frederick, who said disdainfully, "Everyone? Certainly not in the circles in which *I* move."

His lofty conviction implied to Lucinda that if one was not one of Frederick's intimates, then one was completely beyond the pale.

Lady Waverley inquired faintly, "But, Robert, wherever did you buy such a strange garment?"

This was the question Lucinda had been dreading. Robert said airily, "Oh, I sent to London and had them made."

Lord Waverley raised an eloquent bushy eyebrow. The entire family was quite well aware that until he was twenty-one, Robert had no money of his own. On the meager allowance apportioned him by the Earl, the younger son could not possibly afford to have clothes made by expensive London tailors.

The silence lengthened. The only sound was that of Lady Waverley, nervously tapping her diamond ring on the polished side table.

At last Lucinda could bear it no longer. With a defiant tilt to her head, she declared boldly, "To own the truth, Papa, I made the trowsers for Robert. He showed me a picture of the Czar and I copied them from that. It was only meant in jest."

Lord Waverley looked fit to explode. But before he could erupt, Melanie suddenly slumped in her chair. "Oh, dear," she murmured, "I feel so faint. Lucinda, could I trouble you to assist me to my chamber?"

Immediately, the family was all concern.

"It must be the heat of the fire," proclaimed Lord Waverley.

"No, it was probably the strain of the long journey," declared Frederick.

Lady Waverley kept her opinion to herself. Suddenly, she had forgotten her worries about the oyster sauce, and even those appalling trowsers of Robert's. Melanie had been married now for three months. Could it be . . . ? As Lucinda led the dark-haired girl from the drawing room, Lady Waverley took up her petit point, her mind a-whirl as she contemplated the renovation of the nursery, the preparation of the layette, the joy of having a baby in the family again.

Once they had ascended the stairs and were approaching Melanie's chamber in the guest wing, Lady Alford gently disengaged herself from Lucinda's arm.

"I am not really faint, Lucinda. I merely thought it timely to create a diversion, that's all."

Lucinda laughed. "I am most grateful to you. Though by the contemplative expression in Mama's eyes just now, you are going to have a hard time convincing her that her longed-for grandchild is not on the way!"

Melanie smiled sweetly. "There is plenty of time for children. I intend to have at least six. Do come into my apartments for a moment, sister. I have something for you."

As Lucinda followed Melanie through into the dressing room, she noted with approval that a maid had already finished the unpacking.

Melanie handed Lucinda a small parcel. Lucinda tore off the wrapping and exclaimed with delight as she gazed on an exquisite etui case, fashioned in lilac jasper and gold. "Oh, how beautiful!" she exclaimed.

Melanie said, a trifle drily, "It will be ideal to keep your scissors and spare needles in, next time you are called upon to do some sewing for Robert! Though, had I realized Robert was such a dandy, I would have brought him one of the new twisted glass walking sticks. All the bucks in London are sporting them now."

"It is fortunate that you did not bring such

a thing," commented Lucinda, "for Papa would surely have broken it over his head. Papa is a dear man, and we all love him, but he does deeply resent change, and anything new."

"Whereas Robert is quite the reverse," mused Melanie, sitting at her toilet table and brushing her fine, silky hair.

Lucinda nodded. "He loves to be first with everything. I remember when we were children he screamed himself into a fit until Nanny allowed him to ride in a strange new kind of carriage, which was driven by steam instead of horses."

Melanie wrinkled her pretty nose. "Steam? What an odd idea."

"Oh, yes," said Lucinda. "Even today, Robert will tell you (out of Papa's hearing, of course) that one day all carriages will be driven by steam."

"But what will happen to all the horses?" asked Melanie.

"You must inquire of Robert," laughed Lucinda. "Doubtless he will have an answer for that as well."

Glancing around the dressing room, Lucinda was surprised to see, half tucked out of sight beneath a shawl, some novels by Mrs. Mary Meake.

She could not resist the query, "Why, Melanie, does Frederick really allow you to read such books?"

Melanie flushed. "I must confess, Lucinda, that Frederick is not aware that I read them. While he is busy at the House of Lords, I slip away from Curzon Street and visit the circulating library."

Lucinda was intrigued. "Somehow, I had not imagined *you* enjoying such stories of adventure and romance."

"I love my husband," said Melanie. "He is a good, decent man. I am fortunate to be so well settled, so secure. I am aware that my life has been cossetted and indulged. I know that if I suddenly found myself alone on a heath, confronted by a highwayman, I would die of fright and long to be back in my dear house. But to sit at home, safe and secure, with the curtains drawn and the lamps lit, and read about such adventures is another matter entirely. Then it is thrilling, and I do not feel afraid at all. I suppose you must think me terribly foolish?"

"Of course not," said Lucinda. And she meant it. As she made her way downstairs, she reflected about how much she liked Melanie. She was not particularly vivacious, or the type to put herself forward in any manner, yet she possessed a quiet determination which made Lucinda realize that behind those soft, pansy-like eyes there was a will of steel.

Frederick, mused Lucinda as she reentered the drawing room, you've found yourself quite a match in Melanie!

Much to Lady Waverley's relief, the family dinner that evening passed off without mishap. Robert, who had obediently changed from Cossak trowsers into some more acceptable breeches, was on his best behavior. And Frederick pronounced the dinner excellent, even going so far as to compliment his mother on the piquancy of the oyster sauce.

Nevertheless, Lucinda could see that her mother was glad when the cloth was drawn and she was able to lead the ladies from the room and leave the gentlemen to their port and brandy.

No sooner were the three ladies seated in the drawing room than Lady Waverley turned to Melanie and said fervently, "I feel I must apologize for our rustic dining room furniture. Whatever must you have thought of that antique three-piece sideboard?"

"But it is so practical," replied Melanie tactfully.

Lady Waverley threw up her hands in despair. "We must be the only family in the entire county to own a sideboard in three separate pieces! But Lord Waverley is so old-fashioned, he will not hear of us having one of the newer, compact models."

Lucinda crossed to the round tea table, and picked up the chased silver teapot. "Has Papa always been so conservative?"

"He's inherited the trait from his own father," replied Lady Waverley, smiling as she remembered. "Why, when I was first invited to dine with his family, they were scandalized by the current fashion for what they called *promiscuous seating.*"

Lucinda's eyes widened. "Whatever was that, Mama! It sounds very wicked."

"Oh, it *was*," replied Lady Waverley drolly. "It simply meant a seating arrangement of lady, gentleman, lady, gentleman. The Verneys regarded this as too sinful for words, so we were forced to sit with the gentlemen ranged down one side of the table, with the ladies safely out of reach across from them!"

Melanie was laughing so much she could hardly hold her teacup. "But is it not strange," she commented, "that Frederick appears to have inherited Lord Waverley's preference for the traditional, whereas your younger son has quite the opposite character."

"In truth," said Lucinda, "Frederick and Robert quarreled so much as boys that Papa decided to send them to different schools. Frederick was at Eton, so Robert was sent to Winchester.

"But, of course, it was a total disaster," sighed Lady Waverley. "Another of Robert's *firsts* was to lead a riot against the headmaster."

Melanie's brown eyes were huge with amazement.

Lucinda giggled. "The boys decided the headmaster was far too strict, so they mined his study with gunpowder and then made a bonfire of all their desks. Then they retreated to an island in the school grounds, and were only defeated when the militia were called in!"

"At which juncture," said Lady Waverley severely, "Robert was removed from the school and despatched to Eton, where Frederick could keep a watchful eye on him."

"And now he has left Eton, what will he do?" inquired Melanie.

"That is a touchy point," admitted Lucinda.

37

"He longs to take a commission in the hussars, but Papa has other plans."

"Did I hear my name?" asked a jovial voice from the door. Lord Waverley, in mellow mood after his port, led in the gentlemen to join the ladies.

No sooner were the menfolk seated than Lord Waverley said to his daughter, "Lucinda, why not show Melanie the picture gallery? I am sure she would find it most interesting."

"But, Papa, I was intending to show Melanie the gallery tomorrow. The light is so much better there during the day."

"Do not argue, Lucinda," put in Frederick. "Obey your father."

Reluctantly, Lucinda rose to her feet. How unfair, she thought rebelliously. Why should I be sent out of this warm, cozy room to walk up and down in that cold, drafty gallery? She glanced at her sister, hoping for some support, but Melanie's eyes were cast demurely down.

As they mounted the oak staircase toward the gallery, Lucinda murmured, "I am so sorry about this, Melanie. Sometimes Papa and Frederick make me feel about twelve years old!"

Melanie was quite composed. "Don't worry, sister. To tell the truth, I was seeking an excuse to retire early. Perhaps, when you return to the drawing room, you would be so good as to explain that walking around the gallery has fatigued me and I have gone to my room?"

Lucinda smiled. Clever Melanie. Why am I not like you, outwardly demure, yet quietly taking advantage of each situation to suit your own ends?

But that is not my nature, reflected Lucinda ruefully. I am far more impetuous. I have to speak my mind, even if it costs me dear. And I cannot be content, like Melanie, to sit at home and read about adventures. I want to experience them! I should not be afraid if a highwayman confronted me on a lonely heath. At least, I should not fear, provided it was a certain gentleman of the night. . . .

She let out a long sigh as they entered the gallery. It was, in fact, a splendid place, crammed with pictures, statues, and bronzes brought back by several generations of Verneys after their Grand Tours. Here, too, were hung the Verney family portraits, many of which were several hundred years old. Lucinda shivered, uneasily conscious of generations of disapproving blue Verney eyes staring down at her.

Oh, how trapped I feel! Does no one realize, or care, that instead of walking sedately along this gallery with Melanie, I would love to run and turn a cartwheel at the end!

But still the blue Verney eyes regarded her sternly from the walls. All except one, that is, a painting of an unnamed girl. The portrait had always fascinated Lucinda, for the girl it featured did not have the blue Verney eyes, but eyes that were the same color as Lucinda's own —a deep, lustrous amethyst.

The mystery girl was dressed in blue, and the artist had caught her with a lively expression on her face, as if in the act of defiantly tossing her golden curls. Instinctively, Lucinda knew that of all her ancestors, the girl in blue was the only one who would understand the restless spirit that possessed her.

Melanie's low, sweet voice broke into her thoughts. "I imagine the family wanted us out of the way while they discussed Robert's future."

Lucinda nodded. "Poor Robert. Now if this were one of our novels, Melanie, he would run away to join the Army and cover himself in glory in the French war. But this is real life, not a fairytale. Regrettably, Robert has no money of his own. Certainly not enough to buy himself a commission."

Melanie said thoughtfully, "But surely he would feel it his duty to stay and assist your father, if Lord Waverley found the estate too much to manage by himself?"

"If that were the case, then naturally Robert would stay," replied Lucinda. "But Papa is fit and healthy. He adores managing the estate. If Robert were to help, they would have different ideas about every single thing, and the quarrels would be endless."

"In most families it is the accepted custom for younger sons to enter the Army," mused Melanie.

"Unfortunately for Robert," replied Lucinda, "the Army has never been a traditional career for Verney younger sons. And although the estate will in time revert to Frederick, Papa is aware that your husband will be content to reside in London for the major part of the year."

Melanie nodded. "He takes his Parliamentary responsibilities very seriously."

"So you see, it would eventually be a great

help to Frederick if Robert was trained to manage the estate in his absence."

"And yet . . ." sighed Melanie, "I cannot help feeling that before he settles down, Robert should be given his freedom. Anyone can see that he is plagued by a wild, untamed spirit."

Lucinda gave Melanie a sharp glance. "Is a restless spirit always that obvious in a person?" she probed.

"Oh, I am always able to sense it when it is present." Then Melanie went on, with scarcely a second's pause, "But what about you, Lucinda?"

Lucinda was startled. Had Melanie guessed something of her inner turmoil? "What . . .what do you mean?" she hedged.

Melanie smiled. "You are so concerned about Robert's future. But what of your own? After all, in London, any girl as beautiful as yourself would have been married years ago."

"I have no desire to marry yet awhile," said Lucinda lightly. "Besides, living in the country as we do, I have few opportunities to meet eligible gentlemen."

"It is a vexing situation," said Melanie slowly, "especially as I suspect that no ordinary man will do for you, Lucinda."

"What do you mean?" queried Lucinda. Really, she thought, I must stop asking Melanie what she means all the time! But then, Melanie was proving to be an intriguingly perceptive girl.

"I am saying that you are no ordinary girl," said Melanie, with quiet conviction. "You have beauty and charm. But so have a score of others. What makes you exceptional is your joyful vivacity. You are not like the rest of us. You, above all, need a strong man who will understand and enjoy that singular wild spirit of yours."

Lucinda had a torrent of questions to ask, but Melanie, maddeningly, would say no more. She kissed her sister good night, and went to bed, leaving Lucinda's mind in a complete whirl.

After a respectable interval had elapsed, Lucinda rejoined her family in the drawing room. Whatever the secret topic had been during her absence, conversation was now general: the progress of the war in Europe . . . the new fashion of sea bathing (Lord Waverley, to no one's surprise was strongly against the idea. "I am not a *duck*," he proclaimed scathingly.)

Yet despite the light, civilized talk, to Lucinda the atmosphere in the elegant room was thicker than clotted cream. When Robert sauntered across to the supper table, laden with ham, chicken pie, and his favorite orange fruit jelly, and declared with a yawn, "I confess, I am not at all hungry tonight. If you will excuse me, Mama, I would like to retire early," then Lucinda knew for certain that something serious had occurred to upset him.

Whenever Robert uttered those words, and covered his yawn with his left hand instead of his right, he was sending a message to Lucinda saying: *I must talk to you. Meet me in the old nursery as quickly as possible!*

Robert made his escape, but for Lucinda it was not so easy. Frederick had embarked on a long dissertation about how he would solve the traffic congestion in London. All wheeled vehicles, he explained, should only be allowed to travel one way down each street, thus preventing the collisions and jams for which London was so notorious.

Lord Waverley muttered that this was all very well, but the young bucks would no doubt regard it as great sport to ride their phaetons the wrong way down a street, just to prove what dashing young blades they were.

The minutes dragged by. During a lull in the conversation, Lucinda seized her chance, and rose to her feet. But before she could excuse herself, Lady Waverley said, "Lucinda dear, while you are up, would you pass me my workbasket? I want you to help me choose the embroidery silks for a new firescreen. I was tempted by a pink and lilac color scheme, but Melanie hinted earlier that white and black is all the mode in London now. What is your opinion?"

Lucinda repressed a sigh. She fetched the workbasket and gently hurried her mother into choosing the black and white silks, enlivened with a touch of terra-cotta.

At last, she was free to say good night. She walked with slow, easy grace from the room, conscious of her father's critical eyes appraising her excellent deportment.

The moment the drawing room doors were closed behind her, she lifted her skirt and ran upstairs, through galleries and long passages, until she reached the room which had once been the Verney children's day nursery.

Robert was already there, busy lighting candles to brighten the gloom. "Why were you so long?"

"I came as quickly as I could." Lucinda sneezed. "My, it's dusty in here. It is an age since we met in the nursery like this, Robert. I had quite forgotten how lovely and cozy it is. Like another world . . ."

She took a candle and wandered round the nursery, remembering with nostalgia and affection the happy days of her childhood. "Look, Robert, there is our old rocking horse!"

"And my whipping top!" exclaimed Robert. "How proud I was of that."

Lucinda stumbled against an object which squeaked as it fell over. "Why, it is the baby carriage, squeaking because the wheels need oiling. See, Nanny tied a toy bird to it, to amuse us when we were babies. Oh, and look," she ran her hand along the bookshelves, "all my old favorites are here. *Cinderella, Sleeping Beauty,* and *Gulliver's Travels.* Do you remember how Mama came to read us a story at bedtime?"

Robert took her hand and pulled her down beside him on a pile of cushions on the floor. "Those days are long past," he said gravely. "Now we are grown up. Papa feels it is time we both took our place in the world."

Lucinda's eyes were huge with compassion. "Oh, Robert, is that what the talk was about this evening? I have no doubt you were refused permission to join the Army, and told you must stay here instead and manage the estate with Papa."

"That's about the size of it," said Robert. "Frederick, of course, supported Papa. Mama did her best for me, but at heart she does not want me to leave and go to the war. So it seems that my fate is sealed."

"I am so sorry, Robert. You know if there was anything I could do . . ."

Robert pressed her arm. "I know, my dearest sister. But you must save your sympathy for yourself. For it was not only my future that was under discussion this evening."

Lucinda's throat tightened. "They were talking about me?"

Robert nodded. "Sister, there is no time to break this to you gently. Papa has decided that it is time for you to marry. Accordingly, Frederick has found you a beau."

"Who is he?" asked Lucinda, with dread.

"His name is Charles Somerford. He is an extremely wealthy man with vast estates in Derbyshire," said Robert, trying to sound encouraging.

Lucinda was not deceived. "What age is he?"

"I am not exactly sure," Robert hedged. "But Frederick did mention that he is a widower. A *rich* widower."

"But not titled?" inquired Lucinda dryly. "I am surprised at Papa, allowing me to wed such a man."

"This is where the matter becomes complicated," said Robert. "There is a title in the Somerford family, which Mr. Charles Somerford is confident of inheriting. But there are many legal tangles to be unravelled first. I'm afraid I didn't listen to that part of it—I was too sunk in gloom over my own future."

"I understand," whispered Lucinda. "Did you happen to hear when I am to have the privilege of meeting our rich widower from Derbyshire?"

Robert swallowed. "Tomorrow."

"Really," laughed Lucinda, her natural sense of humor asserting itself, "Papa is not wasting any time, is he?"

"Charles Somerford will be staying with Lady Falconbridge, and will wait on us tomorrow afternoon. Officially, he will be calling on his acquaintance, Frederick, but—"

"In truth he will be eyeing the prize lamb!"

Robert plucked moodily at the curtain sash. "So there we are. Both of us sunk."

"No!" declared Lucinda vehemently. "We must not give in. I realized that at the moment, the prospects for both of us seem hopeless. But we can fight!" She dragged her brother to his feet, her eyes fiery with determination. "We'll make a pact, Robert, you and I."

Holding his hands in hers, Lucinda went on, "Somehow, we will set ourselves free. I will help you to attain your dream if, when the time comes, you will help me reach mine. Do you agree?"

"I do!" he said fervently. "Oh, Lucinda, I declare you are the bravest, most wonderful sister any fellow could wish for."

She reached up and kissed him on the chin.

"Well, your brave sister is now about to retire for the night. I fancy I shall need all my energy and courage to face our wealthy widower tomorrow!"

THREE

"Papa, how splendid you look!" exclaimed Lucinda as she crossed the cobbled stableyard of Waverley Hall.

Lord Waverley did indeed cut a fine dash in his scarlet hunting coat, immaculately cut breeches, and highly polished riding boots. Frederick and Robert were mounted beside him. Robert's horse stood eighteen hands high, and the groom was tying a bright red ribbon around his tail, as a warning to other riders to keep clear of this powerful, temperamental animal.

Around the horses frisked the hounds, bright-eyed, wet-nosed, and impatient for the day's sport to begin.

Lucinda handed the menfolk glasses of

spiced punch and murmured, "Oh, how I envy you! I wish you would allow me to join the hunt, Papa. Just this once. I promise not to get in the way!"

Robert immediately lent her his support. "Lucinda rides exceptionally well, sir, for a girl."

Lord Waverley downed his punch in one gulp and said disparagingly, "Now, Lucinda, you know full well it is foolhardy and dangerous for a sidesaddle rider to go galloping at fences."

Lucinda lowered her eyes. She dared not tell her father that Robert had taught her to ride a horse cross-saddle, just like a man. She could ride bareback, too. But unfortunately, Lucinda reflected wryly, this was not an accomplishment likely to impress Lord Waverley.

"Besides," Frederick was declaring soberly, "it is hardly seemly for ladies to be seen hunting."

"Stuff!" proclaimed a booming voice behind him. Even the hounds scattered as the indomitable Lady Falconbridge cantered up on her large grey. "What were you saying, Viscount Alford?" she demanded.

Lucinda bit her lip, enjoying the rare spectacle of Frederick discomposed. Rallying, he turned to Lady Falconbridge, who had ridden over from the adjoining estate specially to join the hunt. "Naturally, my lady, I was not referring to a rider of your excellence and experience."

"I should dashed well hope not!" roared the

lady, her florid face framed by an extraordinary plumed hat. "I'll have you know I am related to the Marchioness of Salisbury, Master of the Hatfield Hunt."

All England, mused Lucinda, had heard of the indefatigable Marchioness. No matter that she was now losing her sight and had to be tied onto her horse. She could still out-ride and out-wit any gentleman in the field.

Frederick inclined his head. "Your family has a fine tradition of horsemanship, my lady. But Lucinda, I fear, is too young and inexperienced—"

"Frederick, I'm not!" Lucinda burst out.

"Of course she is not," Lady Falconbridge agreed. "Lord Waverley, it is my opinion that your daughter should have her chance. She could ride alongside me. No trouble."

Lucinda's hopes rose. She held her breath as she gazed up at her father. He might consider Lady Falconbridge's house pretentious in the extreme, but when forced to come face to face with the lady, even Lord Waverley had been known to lose much of his notorious bluster.

But today Lord Waverley was not to be swayed. "Unfortunately, Lucinda has many other things to occupy her today. Besides, should anyone call, I would be ashamed to see my daughter appearing flushed and dishevelled from the hunt."

Anyone being Mr. Charles Somerford, thought Lucinda grimly.

Lord Waverley went on, "Now, do not let us

detain you, Lucinda. I believe your mother has asked you to take some brawn down to one of the tenants?"

"Yes, Papa."

Frederick nodded his approval. "It is heartwarming to see you upholding the traditions of a lady, Lucinda. The original meaning of the word *lady*, you know, is *giver of bread*."

Robert rolled his eyes.

Lady Falconbridge laid a sympathetic hand on Lucinda's shoulder. "Never mind, my dear. You shall ride with the hunt some other time." Then, raising her voice, she cried, "Are we all set? Then tally ho!"

"Just a moment, Lady Falconbridge," said the Earl testily. "Kindly remember that *I* am Master of the Hunt. *I* shall give the command to commence."

"Then let's have it!" boomed Lady Falconbridge, slapping her crop against her sturdy thigh. "Else the fox will be over the hills and far away."

Wistfully, Lucinda watched them canter away, the frisky hunters scaring the peacocks strutting on the wide sweep of front lawn.

"One day," she vowed, "I *shall* ride to hounds. And I shall acquit myself so well that soon every gentleman in the county will be proud to accompany me!"

Meanwhile, there was her duty to be done. She found Mrs. Trotter, the wife of one of the farmworkers, sitting with her bandaged foot resting on a stool. She was clearly very pleased to see the Lady Lucinda, though agitated that her injury prevented her from rising and offering her guest proper refreshment.

"You'll find a jug of my special homemade ale on the dresser, my lady," she said, in her soft country burr. "I'd be proud to offer you some, but I can't rise to my feet."

"Let me pour some for us both," offered Lucinda. She was not, in fact, at all partial to ale, but realized that it would be most impolite for her to refuse.

As she fetched the rough, earthenware tankards, she glanced around with approval at the little farm cottage. She had already observed that the outside thatching was neat, and the walls and windows were in a good state of repair. She felt a touch of pride at this evidence of her father's concern for his tenants. He may set high standards for others, she thought, but he is strict with himself, too. He takes his responsibilities toward his tenants seriously.

And here in the warm, cozy kitchen, Mrs. Trotter obviously took a pride in keeping everything pin-neat. Lucinda had seen cottages on other estates, where the floor was smeared with a mixture of soot and ale, to hide the dirt. But Mrs. Trotter had fresh, sweet-smelling rushes strewn on the floor, and her pots and pans on the range were burnished bright.

"How are your children, Mrs. Trotter?" Lucinda inquired, drawing up a stool.

"They are a great comfort to me, my lady. I am a truly lucky woman. Why, even the youngest bring home a few coppers each week, hard earned by stone-picking in the fields, or scaring the birds from the crops. And my eldest, Tom, has two jobs now. In the afternoons he sees to the cows, and then at night he keeps watch at Medlow Grange."

"Is that not the ruined house just beyond Medlow Woods?" asked Lucinda. "I must confess I have ever been intrigued by the place, but my father always forbade me to go there. He would never tell me why!"

Mrs. Trotter shook her head. "It's no place for the likes of a lady such as you." She lowered her voice. "They say the Grange is haunted."

Lucinda's eyes widened. "A ghost! How exciting!"

"I'm surprised you know so little about it," went on Mrs. Trotter, "seeing as how the ghost is a distant ancestor of yours."

"Of mine! Oh, Mrs. Trotter, please tell me more."

Anxiety clouded the older woman's eyes. "I don't know if your father would want me to, my lady."

"Please," pleaded Lucinda. "I promise you I will never reveal to him what I know, or who told me."

Mrs. Trotter was easily convinced. In truth, there was nothing she liked better than to sit beside her kitchen range and recount the strange stories of her neighborhood.

She picked up an unfinished patchwork quilt and began to sew on a bright red square. "'Tis a sad tale, my lady. The girl involved was the Lady Ellen Fitzjohn. Her mother was a

Verney, so that's how you come to be related. Well, the story goes that she was being forced to marry a man she loathed. He was titled, and rich, but she hated him. And in the meantime, she was planning to elope with her true love, a dashing but penniless young man."

Lucinda sat rapt. "Go on," she urged softly.

"The lovers had arranged to meet in the summer house of the Grange and run away from there," said Mrs. Trotter. "But on the appointed night, Ellen's father got wind of the scheme. He blazed into the summer house, caught the pair in the act of an embrace, and sliced into the young man with his sword, killing him in seconds."

"Oh, how terrible!"

"Worse was to come," said Mrs. Trotter grimly. "The Lady Ellen was so distraught, she seized the sword from her lover's poor, bleeding body, and flung herself upon the point, running it straight through her heart."

Lucinda could hardly speak. Oh, how she felt for that poor, doomed girl! "That is the most tragic story I have ever heard," she whispered.

Mrs. Trotter nodded. "Her father was grief-stricken, and overcome with remorse. He died himself not long after. But in his will, he decreed that the summer house must always be guarded, and that no one must ever enter it again. I don't know if it's true, but it is rumored that Ellen hid some gold there, which she was planning to take with her when she eloped."

"And the ghost?" asked Lucinda.

Mrs. Trotter snapped off her thread and smoothed out the patchwork. "Legend has it that on scented spring nights, Ellen returns, searching for her lover and the happiness she should have known. But my Tom will have none of it. He's a fearless lad, and says that on all the nights he's been keeping watch, there's never been sight of a ghost."

"Poor, tortured Ellen," sighed Lucinda. "I wonder what she looks like?"

"She was supposed to be very beautiful," said Mrs. Trotter, sipping her ale, "with golden hair and fine eyes, the same pale violet shade as your own."

Lucinda flushed with excitement. Of course! That mysterious, unnamed portrait in the picture gallery! It must be Ellen Fitzjohn. It could be no one else. The lively, spirited expression and defiant toss of the head were now explained. Lucinda was positive that the portrait must have been painted as Ellen was making her plans to elope!

Reluctantly, Lucinda rose to her feet. "What a fascinating tale, Mrs. Trotter. I am only sorry I cannot stay longer, but Mama will be expecting me home."

"It's good of you to spare the time to come, my lady," smiled Mrs. Trotter. "You'll be sure to thank Lady Waverley for the brawn, won't you?"

Outside the cottage, Lucinda paused to admire Mrs. Trotter's neat little kitchen garden. Lucinda had a lively curiosity, and was particularly interested in the pieces of broken glass Mrs. Trotter had placed over the early asparagus plants. Presumably, reasoned Lucinda, to protect the asparagus from the elements and make them grow faster. How clever!

Wandering down the verdant country lane, with her mind still dwelling on the tragic tale of Ellen Fitzjohn, Lucinda suddenly realized that she had walked to the exact spot near the hawthorn hedge where those ruffians had attacked her night before last.

Night before last! Had her adventure really started so short a time ago? She strolled down the lane, her heart beating faster as she recalled her gallant stranger riding to her rescue, and carrying her off through the night. And here, outside Dr. Webster's house, he had set her down. Here he had kissed her hand and told her he was her friend.

Lucinda closed her eyes, trying to relive the episode, to experience once again the surge of elation and excitement she had felt with the masked man. But it was no longer a balmy spring night. Instead, the bright sunshine pricked her eyelids, and Dr. Webster's gate was banging in the wind, driving her precious memory away.

Lucinda sighed. How foolish I am, she thought sadly, to dwell so much on the incident. Why, my mysterious stranger is no doubt miles away by now, and for sure has forgotten all about me. It is highly unlikely that I shall ever see him again. I must put him out of my mind. I must think ahead, to my meeting with Mr. Charles Somerford this afternoon.

Yet despite her resolution to be sensible and realistic, Lucinda was powerless to curb her soaring imagination. If this were one of Mrs. Mary Meake's novels, she mused, then Charles Somerford would stride into the drawing room this afternoon . . . I should look up, all fear and trepidation, and find to my delight that he was none other than my mysterious stranger!

But of course, that would be too convenient a solution. Regrettably, Lucinda realized, life was never as simple as that! Nevertheless, being incurably optimistic by nature, it did occur to her that she may have formed completely the wrong opinion of Charles Somerford.

After all, she thought, here am I condemning the gentleman before I have even set eyes on him. Just because someone as sober as Frederick approves of Mr. Somerford, it does not mean he will necessarily prove to be a dull clod. Why, he might be dashing, handsome, adventurous . . . everything I've ever dreamed of in a man.

And yet, despite her determination to face the future with sense and courage, Lucinda could not resist a final backward glance to the place by Dr. Webster's house where her gallant man of the night had reached out and kindled such a flame of restless longing within her.

Gilbert the footman coughed discreetly at the drawing room doors. "My lady, a Mr. Charles Somerford has arrived."

Lady Waverley dropped her sewing and affected an expression of surprise. "Mr. Somerford? Oh, dear . . . Frederick did advise me that a gentleman of that name might be waiting on him this afternoon. And now he has come before the menfolk have returned from the hunt. How vexing!"

Lucinda stubbornly refused to meet Lady Waverley's eye. If her mother was determined to persist in this charade of pretending that Mr. Somerford had come to call on Frederick, then Lucinda was equally determined to play no part in the scene. It had amused her to notice that Lady Waverley had been increasingly agitated all day, and the stitches on her new firescreen had become more and more ragged as the time approached for Mr. Somerford to pay his *surprise* call.

When Lucinda failed to respond, Lady Waverley turned to Melanie, who was quietly occupied with scissors and black paper, making a silhouette picture. "Melanie, are you acquainted with Mr. Somerford?"

From Melanie's genuinely perplexed expression, Lucinda realized that Frederick had not confided the family plans for his sister and Mr. Somerford. "We have been introduced, but our meeting was brief," she said.

"Well," fluttered Lady Waverley, "it would be most discourteous to leave the gentleman standing in the hall. We must endeavor to entertain him until Frederick returns. Gilbert, kindly admit him."

As Gilbert adjusted his wig, and left the room, Lady Waverley whispered, "Lucinda. Your hair is looking wispy. Quickly, tidy it up."

Lucinda repressed a smile as she crossed gracefully to the mirror above the marble fireplace to smooth down her unruly curls. Oh, Mr. Somerford, she thought wryly, have you any notion of the consternation you have caused in this country drawing room?

"Mr. Charles Somerford," intoned Gilbert.

Lucinda closed her eyes. Please, she prayed, *please* let him be at least reasonably acceptable!

She forced herself to gaze on the man bowing low over her mother's ringed hand. A leaden weight seemed to settle around her heart. Of course, he was not her mysterious stranger. That would have been too much to hope for. But neither was he dashing, handsome—or even particularly young.

Charles Somerford was a stocky man of average height, in his middle thirties Lucinda judged, with thinning lank brown hair, a coarse-grained face and thick, fleshy lips.

I cannot marry him, she thought wildly. I *cannot!*

Lucinda steeled herself not to squirm as he took her hand and bowed. She dipped him the briefest of curtseys and favored him with a glance of complete indifference. On no account, she resolved, must he believe me to be a willing party to this match.

"I am only sorry that my husband and sons are not here to greet you," said Lady Waverley, vaguely waving her hands and looking guilty, as if, Lucinda thought, she had deliberately concealed the menfolk behind the long silk window curtains.

Charles Somerford's pale eyes gleamed. "Indeed, my lady, I am charmed to find myself in the company of three delightful ladies. Lady Alford, it is a particular pleasure to renew my acquaintance with you."

"Oh, yes," smiled Melanie, "I believe we

were introduced at my house on Curzon Street."

"That is so," said Mr. Somerford, "but I have also passed you near Hill Street on one occasion. You were just leaving the circulating library, but regrettably did not appear to recognize me."

Melanie paled. "Why, no, Mr. Somerford. To be sure, you must be mistaken. I do not frequent the circulating library!"

Lucinda had determined not to utter a word to Charles Somerford. But now it was evident that Melanie required her help—and speedily. Accordingly, Lucinda settled herself next to Lady Waverley on the sofa, and inquired, "Do you reside in London, Mr. Somerford?"

He shook his head, causing a strand of lank hair to fall across his lined brow. "Indeed not, Lady Lucinda. I have a large estate in Derbyshire which requires my attention for most of the year. But I am required to visit the capital from time to time on business. Lord Alford and I share the same London banker, which is how we happen to be acquainted."

"And how fortunate," said Lucinda sweetly, "that you should *happen* to be visiting this remote part of the country, just when my brother is paying us a visit."

If Charles Somerford detected the acid undernote to her tone, he was careful not to reveal it as he replied, "I have the honor to be staying with Lady Falconbridge, at Brent Park."

Lucinda could not resist goading him further. "Then I am surprised you did not join her ladyship on the hunt today."

Out of the corner of her eye, Lucinda observed her mother creasing and uncreasing her lace handkerchief. Poor Mama! She was clearly frantic in case it came to light that Mr. Somerford's call was no casual incident.

Fortunately for Charles Somerford, he was saved the need to reply. The doors burst open and the menfolk surged into the room, bullishly ebullient after their day's sport.

"Wily old fox got away," declared Lord Waverley, "but we gave him a good run!"

As Charles Somerford rose to his feet, Frederick stepped forward and made the introductions. Then he said, "I am sorry we were not here to receive you, Somerford. But I trust the ladies have been keeping you entertained."

Never one to be subtle, Frederick cast an inquiring glance at Lucinda. She stared back at him, frostily.

"Indeed," murmured Charles Somerford, "your delightful sister has almost made me feel one of the family."

Lucinda nearly choked. Robert, in total sympathy with his sister, hastily turned away and affected an earnest study of Melanie's silhouette picture.

Really, fumed Lucinda, this was carrying matters too far! One of the family, *indeed!*

To her horror, she heard her father asking their guest if he would do them the honor of dining at Waverley Hall that evening. It came as no surprise to anyone to learn that Mr. Somerford was not, in fact, engaged to dine elsewhere that day, and so the matter was fixed.

Over dinner, Lucinda contrived to say as little to Mr. Somerford as was politely possible. She was highly relieved when at last the cloth was removed and Lady Waverley gave the signal for the ladies to withdraw.

Yet within fifteen minutes, the gentlemen appeared in the drawing room. Lucinda irritably poured the tea, reflecting that her father was losing no opportunity to throw her and Mr. Somerford together. She had never known him take less than an hour over his port and brandy before.

Lord Waverley rubbed his hands. "Isn't this pleasant," he declared genially. "We rarely have visitors, Mr. Somerford. I have said to Lady Waverley quite often that we must entertain more regularly. We are inclined to become dull, you know, living so quietly in the country."

Even the loyal Lady Waverley could not bring herself to utter a word in support of this blatant fiction.

Charles Somerford leaned forward and commented, "Sir, in my experience country life can be just as much a social whirl as it is in London. Indeed, Lady Falconbridge informed me only this morning that she is planning a large masked ball. I trust you and your family will be honoring the event with your presence?"

Lucinda lowered her eyes, lest her father should witness the glimmer of amusement shining from them. The odious Charles Somerford had caught him out! Normally, Lord Waverley discouraged all visits to Lady Falconbridge's despised house. But now he was trapped, like a fly on a pin.

Lord Waverley squirmed in his chair. "Ah . . . a masked ball, you say?"

"That sounds a merry do! I've no doubt all the county will be there," put in Robert, grinning faintly.

"Yes . . . well, no doubt we shall all attend. Why not?" said Lord Waverley, sounding slightly dazed. "Now, Lucinda, I am sure it would please our guest if you played for us on the harpsichord."

Charles Somerford nodded. "How delightful to see a harpsichord once more in a drawing room. Its tone is so much sweeter than these newer pianofortes."

Lord Waverley looked pleased. "Never could get on with the pianoforte. We have one in the music room, of course, but I have always encouraged my daughter to play the harpsichord, and the harp."

"And you must sing to us, too, Lucinda," insisted Lady Waverley as Lucinda seated herself at the instrument. "She has the most charming voice, Mr. Somerford."

He smiled. "Indeed, I have no doubt that the Lady Lucinda is *the* most accomplished young lady."

Lucinda ignored him. Perhaps, she thought fervently, as she ran her fingers over the keys, perhaps Charles Somerford is merely being civil. It may be that secretly he is disappointed in me, and has changed his mind about marriage. Oh, please let him return speedily to Lady Falconbridge, and not bother calling here again!

But there was to be no avoiding the rich widower from Derbyshire. The following day Frederick and Robert had arranged for Mr. Somerford to join them in a ride over to Guildford, to inspect a new hunter. Lucinda was invited to make up the party.

"It is very kind of you, Frederick, but I would only slow you down if I rode with you," Lucinda demurred.

"Nonsense," Frederick said with a frown, "Why, only yesterday you were saying how much you would like to join us on the hunt. Now I am offering you the opportunity of a gallop, and here you are, all of a dither. Kindly be ready by eleven o'clock."

Lucinda said, a trifle wildly, "Perhaps Melanie would care to accompany us—"

"Melanie and I have various household matters to discuss," interrupted Lady Waverley. "She will be quite content to have a quiet day here with me, whilst you enjoy a pleasant outing with your brothers . . . and Mr. Somerford, of course. Oh, and Lucinda, be sure to wear your new riding habit. After all, you will want your *brothers* to be proud of you."

Indeed, thought Lucinda.

When Lucinda and her brothers met with Charles Somerford on the outskirts of Brent Park, she deduced from the admiring expression in his pale blue eyes that her appearance gave him every satisfaction. Her dark green riding habit was exquisitely cut, and it revealed her trim figure to perfection. She had completed her ensemble with black half-boots, tan leather gloves, and a smart beaver hat, decorated with ostrich feathers.

It was a glorious day, with fluffy white clouds scudding across the blue sky, swept by a fresh breeze which soon brought a flattering flush to Lucinda's dazzling complexion. She was mounted on her favorite chestnut mare, and noticed with some amusement that Frederick and Robert had drawn a little ahead, clearly to give her and Mr. Somerford the opportunity to become better acquainted.

Charles Somerford lost no time in opening the conversation.

"Very pretty countryside this," he remarked, surveying the gentle green hills and winding lanes south of Guildford. "But I must confess, I feel more at home in my native Derbyshire. The landscape there has a more rugged quality. Tell me, Lady Lucinda, are you at all acquainted with that part of the world?"

"I regret not," replied Lucinda coolly. "Though if you find Derbyshire so attractive, Mr. Somerford, no doubt you will be anxious to return there?"

He gave her a frank glance. She looked into his fishy, pale eyes and quickly averted her head. Oh, he was the most coarse-looking man! Yet it was not merely his appearance which repulsed her. Instinctively, she was conscious of something else . . . something lurking and evil about this man which sent a shiver right through her, although she was already warm from the ride.

Charles Somerford, blissfully unaware of Lucinda's loathing, continued placidly: "I shall not return to Derbyshire until my business here is successfully concluded. My first wife, Anna, died a year ago. To be blunt, it is no secret that I am seeking a replacement."

"Really?" said Lucinda disdainfully.

He paid no heed to the distaste in her tone. "I am sensible of precisely the type of girl I require. Anna was a loyal wife—unfortunately, we were not blessed with children—but she was rather on the solid side, and, well, even her mother owned that she was somewhat plain. For the next Mrs. Somerford, I've a mind to choose a more lively girl. She must be healthy and strong, of course, but I should prefer her to possess more than her fair share of good looks."

Beneath the beaver hat, Lucinda's fine eyes were fiery with indignation. Merciful heavens, anyone would think he was in the market for a horse . . . she must have good teeth, a sound disposition, glossy coat, and lively eyes!

Clearly interpreting her silence as becoming modesty, Mr. Somerford continued, "I have a great deal to offer the right lady. I enjoy a sizable income, and when the legal tangles are resolved, I am confident of inheriting the title of Duke of Lexburgh."

"I should have imagined," said Lucinda icily, "that to search for a wife here in the country would be a sad waste of your time. There must be a score of eligible ladies in London who would be only too delighted to compete for the prospects you have to offer."

"No," said Mr. Somerford firmly, "I desire no simpering London miss. I need a wife who understands the ways of the country. And I am not prepared to invest a great deal of my time in the search. Certainly, I have no plans to act the Court dandy in the capital."

Lucinda's smile was glacial. The man

seemed totally lacking in subtlety. His intentions were only too clear. It was as if he had allotted himself a limited amount of time to complete his matrimonial business . . . within weeks, it seemed, the bargain would be struck, contracts enchanged, and the hapless bride bundled up to Derbyshire as if she were a prize bale of wool.

For the remainder of the journey, Lucinda conversed with Mr. Somerford in the curtest of tones, refusing to advance one jot of information about herself. No, she had never had the pleasure of visiting Brighton. Yes, she did understand that the Prince Regent had made it the most fashionable place. Yes, Lady Falconbridge's forthcoming masked ball did sound quite exciting. No, she had never ridden to hounds. Yes, many people had been kind enough to tell her that she was a most accomplished horsewoman.

What relief when the little town of Guildford came into sight. Lucinda had imagined that Charles Somerford would desire to view the hunter with her brothers. But to her chagrin, as they approached the stables, Mr. Somerford murmured to Frederick:

"I confess, after my ride I have a longing to walk a while. Would you permit me to escort your charming sister in a stroll beside the river, whilst you complete your business at the stables?"

Lucinda flashed an imploring glance at Robert, who at once attempted her rescue. "Oh, but I am convinced Lucinda would prefer to see the hunter," he said firmly.

But Frederick sided with Mr. Somerford. "No, it occurs to me that a crowd of us viewing the horse might unsettle the animal. Lucinda, you walk for a while with Mr. Somerford, and then you may view the hunter later."

Charles Somerford assisted Lucinda down from her mare. "Come, Lady Lucinda. I have a notion that the river path lies this way. Is it not an enchanting sight, framed by the willow trees?"

As they ambled along the mossy path, Mr. Somerford informed Lucinda further on the matter of his Derbyshire estate. "The Lexburgh estates border mine," he said in his ponderous tone, "so once I inherit the title, my lands will be trebled. I shall be moving, with my bride, into Lexburgh Castle. It is a most imposing residence, much admired and envied by all the county."

Lucinda gazed at the ducks squabbling in the water and said nothing at all.

Suddenly, she felt Charles Somerford's hand on her shoulders, whirling her round to face him. His expression was livid.

"So! Have you nothing to say to me?"

Lucinda was amazed and frightened by his swift change of mood. Nevertheless, she threw back her head and challenged him boldly, "Kindly remove your hands from my riding habit, Mr. Somerford!"

His fingers dug hard into her shoulders. "I do not believe you are shy," he hissed. "I have observed you closely, and I am convinced you are a girl of spirit. Yet with me, you turn away your head, and answer *yes, no, really,* like all the other simpering Surrey misses."

"Release me this instant!" Lucinda demanded, her heart thudding with fear. "Or I shall scream for my brothers."

Charles Somerford's response was to seize her right arm, jerking it painfully up behind her back and rendering her immobile and helpless.

He laughed softly. "But your brothers are back in the stables. There is no one to hear you. No one."

She opened her mouth to scream, but he was too fast for her. He drew her close. To Lucinda's horror, she found his face near hers and his thick, fleshy lips pressing down upon her own.

Nauseated, she kicked and struggled wildly. But he held her fast, searing her pinioned right arm with pain as he covered her cheeks, her mouth with hot, moist kisses.

Lucinda, overcome with repulsion, closed her eyes, convinced she would faint. Just as she knew she could bear it no longer, there came an imperious voice:

"Unhand that lady, you scoundrel!"

Charles Somerford released his grip on Lucinda and spun around. "What the—"

His voice faded as he regarded a tall, powerfully built dark-haired man standing on the path before him. But it was not so much the commanding presence of the newcomer that momentarily silenced Mr. Somerford. It was the fact that the man was wearing a mask.

FOUR

Lucinda shrank back against the willow tree, unable to believe her eyes. She had seen him only once, and then in darkness. But the joyous beating of her heart was like a soaring song of recognition.

Charles Somerford, observing her radiant expression, demanded suspiciously, "Do you know this person, Lady Lucinda?"

"If you have anything to say, kindly address your remarks to me, and refrain from harassing the lady," cut in Lucinda's rescuer.

"Who the devil do you think you are?" blustered the Derbyshire man.

The masked man's voice curled like a whiplash. "I am a gentleman. Which, you, sir, clearly are not!"

"No gentleman of my acquaintance would deem it necessary to hide his countenance beneath a mask," sneered Mr. Somerford. He took a pace forward. "I'll teach you to interfere in my affairs—"

"On the contrary," declared the mysterious stranger icily. "It is you who shall be taught a lesson. You deserve a thrashing for forcing your attentions on a lady in that despicable manner."

Mr. Somerford drew back his fist, and roared, "I'll pulp you!"

He blundered forward, but the masked man was swift and athletic. As the Derbyshire man lunged, the gallant swung his fist and aimed a perfectly timed blow at his opponent's jaw. Charles Somerford staggered, his eyes glazed and rolling. Then he fell, in an unceremonious, unconscious heap, to the ground.

It was only then that Lucinda realized she had been holding her breath. The masked man dusted down his jacket and executed an immaculate bow toward Lucinda.

"I appreciate," he said, in a self-mocking tone, "that the correct and proper behavior would have been to call this creature out to a duel. Regrettably, my time here is limited, so I was forced to resort to fisticuffs."

"I am so grateful," murmured Lucinda, her blood beginning to race as she stared up into the steel-gray eyes of the man in the mask.

He laughed. "You appear to be a lady with a singular talent for adventure. I believe this is the second time I have come upon you struggling to resist the unwanted attentions of a rogue."

Lucinda clasped her hands. "But this time the situation is far worse! When you came to my rescue that night in the lane, my attackers were merely common thieves. But this unspeakable man desires to marry me. And my father seems ready to give his consent!"

"If Charles Somerford is offering for your hand," mused the stranger, crossing his arms before his broad chest, "then I doubt very much if you are a doctor's daughter, as you led me to believe. It is common knowledge that Somerford is angling for a bride with titled parents."

Lucinda flushed. "I did mislead you. I am very sorry. But at the time I was . . . unsure of your motives. I feared that if I named myself as Lucinda Verney, daughter of the Earl of Waverley, you might break into the Hall and steal all our silver."

The man threw back his head and roared with laughter.

Lucinda said indignantly, "It is not such a preposterous notion! Why, the countryside is teeming with rogues." She paused, and then continued in the same spirited vein, "And now, sir, I have revealed my name to you. Is it not time now for you to remove your mask and tell me who you are?"

"Boldly spoken," smiled the man. "I regret, that for the highest of motives, I must remain masked for the present. But I will tell you that my name is Miles."

"And have you mislaid your surname?" Lucinda inquired crisply.

Again that warm, fascinating smile. He had, Lucinda observed, a firm, well-bred mouth—a welcome contrast to Charles Somerford's thick, loose lips.

"For the moment," he said, "you must know me simply as Miles—and ask no further questions."

"Very well," said Lucinda, responding to the authority in his voice. She glanced down at the still unconscious Charles Somerford. "Oh dear, my brothers will be here soon. How am I to explain what has happened? They will never believe that Mr. Somerford made advances toward me, let alone that I was rescued by a masked man, whom I know only as Miles!"

"Tell them," he suggested, "that Mr. Somerford unfortunately tripped over a tree root and knocked his jaw on the willow. I imagine that Charles Somerford himself will support your story. He would not wish to admit that he was bested in such ignoble circumstances."

Lucinda shuddered as she recalled the horror of Charles Somerford's kisses.

"What ails you?" inquired Miles gently.

Lucinda gazed up at him. He was so handsome, and rugged and strong. Why, even the sound of his voice sent tremors running through her. And yet, perhaps because he was masked, she found it easy to converse with him in a manner that would have been most improper with any other gentleman of her acquaintance.

"He made me realize that I can never marry!" she blurted. "If marriage means enduring

. . . that . . . then I must forsake it. Oh, it was too dreadful!"

Miles took her hand. His voice was low as he inquired, "Was that your very first kiss, Lucinda?"

She colored. "Of course. And it will be my last. I am convinced of that."

Miles smiled and looked deep into her eyes. Not for all the world could Lucinda have looked away. His expression was compelling, passionate, and tender all at the same time.

"I think," he said softly, "that one day, at a more convenient time, and in a more romantic place, I shall have to teach you what a joy it is to kiss, Lucinda."

Lucinda felt her blush start somewhere around her waist. Oh, how shameful to permit him to address her like this! And yet, deep in her heart, she knew that if the enchanted time came when Miles should kiss her, then she would prove the most willing pupil.

He lifted her hand and pressed her bare wrist to his lips. "It is time to say farewell," he murmured. "I hear voices, further up the path. No doubt your brothers are searching for you."

"When . . . when shall I see you again?" whispered Lucinda.

He smiled. "Perhaps, sooner than you may imagine."

He bowed, turned, and in an instant had disappeared around a bend in the river path.

For a moment, Lucinda stood staring along the deserted track, unable to believe that she had really encountered him again. Oh, he was the most splendid man! Just to be in his presence aroused the wildest, most heady emotions within her. And he had said that they would meet again, *sooner than you may imagine*.

Exultant at the prospect, Lucinda gazed down on Charles Somerford, who was beginning to rub his face and groan. Hastily, she composed herself and gathered her wits, the better to explain to her brothers how her rich Derbyshire beau came to be lying by a willow tree, with a bump the size of a hen's egg swelling on his jaw.

For Lucinda, the ride back to Waverley seemed interminable. Frederick and Robert had assisted the dazed Charles Somerford to his feet, and thence to his horse. They had accepted Lucinda's explanation of his sorry condition without question, and as the ride commenced were brimful of hearty sympathy for their companion.

"Deuced bad luck, tripping over a tree root like that," declared Frederick.

"Absolutely," agreed Robert. "Could have happened to anyone. You will find a good brisk ride, Mr. Somerford, the ideal thing to clear your head."

As Robert spoke, he cast a sidelong glance at his sister. She fidgeted uncomfortably under his scrutiny. From childhood, Robert had possessed an uncanny sixth sense as far as Lucinda was concerned, and she knew she would have to endure some penetrating questions from her brother as soon as they were alone.

Throughout the ride, Charles Somerford addressed not a word to Lucinda. She was delighted. Had she succeeded in dampening his ardor for her? Did he now consider her an unsuitable candidate for the honor of bearing his name? Surely, decided Lucinda, her spirits rising as she studied Mr. Somerford's averted head, the events of the day must have turned him against her. Oh, how fortunate if he now quitted Surrey and left her alone!

Charles Somerford disguised his coolness toward Lucinda by joining the Verney brothers in their dispute about the hunter they had viewed that morning. Although Mr. Somerford had not himself seen the animal, that in no way prevented him from voicing an opinion on it.

Robert was very much for the horse. "He was lively and full of spirit," he declared. "You would be a fool not to purchase him, Frederick."

Frederick shook his head. "I was disturbed that the groom had just exercised the horse," he said cautiously. "He knew we were coming, and I suspect that he had cantered the hunter deliberately, so we would not realize that the animal was slightly lame."

"Indeed, that is my opinion also," put in Charles Somerford. "It is a fact that certain kinds of lameness are less apparent after exercise."

Lucinda trotted her mare steadily behind the three men, thankful that they were too immersed in their argument to bother with her. When the great iron gates of Brent Park came into view, Charles Somerford slowed his horse and prepared to take his leave. Hopefully, thought Lucinda fervently, this will be the last time I shall set eyes on Charles Somerford. He will make an excuse to Lady Falconbridge and quit Surrey without attending the masked ball. He will trouble me no more!

Charles Somerford removed his hat and politely inclined his head toward Lucinda. "Farewell, then, for the present, Lady Lucinda. It has been a most *instructive* morning. I look forward to renewing our acquaintance at Lady Falconbridge's ball."

Lucinda's heart sank.

"Ah, yes," said Frederick, "the ball. We shall all be attending."

"I am glad," said Mr. Somerford, his pale blue eyes still fixed on Lucinda. "And I give you fair warning, Lady Lucinda, that I intend to claim the first two dances with you. There are so many topics I wish to converse with you about."

Robert laughed. "You forget, Mr. Somerford. It is to be a *masked* ball. How then will you recognize my sister in order to claim your dances?"

"I assure you," said Charles Somerford, "no mask—*whoever* it was worn by—would deter me from my chosen course."

With that, he raised his hand and galloped away. Lucinda shivered. His tone had been bland enough. But she had understood the menace behind his words. The malice in the Derbyshire man's pale blue eyes had sent a chill of foreboding through her bones.

I will never forgive you, those eyes had said. *I shall have my revenge on your masked friend. And I shall make you mine, have no doubt of that.*

78

Back at Waverley Hall, Lucinda changed from her riding habit into a fresh muslin dress and joined her mother and brothers for a light late luncheon. Lord Waverley had taken Melanie for a ride around the estate.

Lucinda desperately wanted to be alone, to reflect on the events of the morning and her encounter with her masked gentleman friend. But this, she realized, was going to be impossible. Already, Robert was making their secret signal indicating that he desired to talk with her privately, while Lady Waverley, across from Lucinda at the dining table, kept raising her eyebrows at her daughter in a manner which indicated that she had certain questions to ask of her.

As the servants cleared away the chicken pie and brought in a lemon *sorbet*, Lucinda excused herself, saying she had eaten her fill and would like to rest after the morning's exercise. She hastened from the room, but to her dismay, Robert followed her.

Holding her arm, he pulled her into a quiet saloon out of earshot of the dining room and hissed, "What happened on the river path today?"

"Happened?" asked Lucinda, wide-eyed. "Whatever do you mean, Robert? Poor Mr. Somerford tripped over a—"

"Stuff!" exclaimed her brother. "I don't believe that tree root nonsense for a moment. We have never had any secrets, Lucinda. Surely you can tell me?"

Lucinda shook her golden head and said softly, "Trust me, Robert. What happened today is something I cannot share with you . . . at the moment. If I could confide in you, I would, you know that."

She felt wretched as she observed his confused, hurt expression. But I cannot even tell my beloved brother, she thought wildly, about Miles and my feelings for him. Why, it is all so new, so bewildering and enthralling that it is hard to find words even to myself to express how I feel when I gaze into Miles's eyes . . . when I see him smile . . . the way I sense I am on fire whenever he so much as kisses my hand.

No, I cannot share him, yet, with any living soul. Just to speak of him would spoil it all for me. After all, this is the first big adventure of my life. To confide, even in someone as dear as Robert, would destroy for me all the magic and excitement.

"Dash it all, sister!" Robert blurted. But before he could continue, the saloon door opened and Lady Waverley entered. Her mouth was set in a determined line, and with no more ado she waved Robert from the saloon, proclaiming that she wished to talk to Lucinda.

When the door had closed behind Robert, Lady Waverley crossed to a brocaded chair, drew her paisley shawl round her shoulders, and inquired, "So, Lucinda. Did you enjoy your ride with your brothers and Mr. Somerford?"

"It was most *instructive*, Mama," murmured Lucinda.

Lady Waverley smiled. "Mr. Somerford seems a most admirable man, does he not? Your father is most impressed with his prospects.

He has a sizable income, you know, and will most surely inherit the title of Duke of Lexburgh. What is more, he is anxious to take back a wife to Derbyshire."

"I know, Mama," said Lucinda drily. "I was interviewed for the position this morning."

Lady Waverley looked taken aback by Lucinda's caustic tone, but inquired pleasantly, "And what is your opinion of Mr. Somerford?"

"I have no wish, Mama," said Lucinda clearly, "to be either Mrs. Charles Somerford *or* the Duchess of Lexburgh."

"Then you are a most foolish and difficult girl," snapped Lady Waverley. "You may never have a chance as good as this again."

"Then I shall cheerfully remain a spinster and devote my life to good works."

Lady Waverley reached for her smelling bottle. "Lucinda," she pleaded, "I must advise you that your father will not take kindly to a refusal of Mr. Somerford. Twice, your father has allowed you to spurn beaux who would have made very good husbands. I fear that this time, he will not be so lenient with you."

Lucinda swallowed. It distressed her to see her mother so upset, and she had no wish to cause friction between her dear parents. She took Lady Waverley's hand. "Do not fret, Mama. Time has a way of solving most of life's problems. And after all, Mr. Somerford has not yet proposed to me. So perhaps we are speaking prematurely."

But as mother and daughter looked at one another, they both knew that the masked ball was fast approaching. This, surely, would be the occasion for Charles Somerford to seek to advance his suit with Lucinda.

Robert, his good humor quickly restored, informed Lucinda the next day that there had been a danger of the Verney family not attending the ball at all.

"Our unsociable father is, as usual, most reluctant to set foot outside the Waverley estate," he told his sister, as they took a morning stroll across the front lawns. "You recollect how he despises Lady Falconbridge's house, and the long flight of steps leading up to the entrance?"

"I do not know why he has taken so against Brent Park," mused Lucinda, the sun making her hair shine like spun gold. "To my mind, the steps lend a certain elegance to the house."

Robert grinned. "Ah, but Papa is convinced that the weather is certain to be inclement and windy when we arrive. He is fearful that by the time we have toiled up the steps we shall all be looking dishevelled and wild as weathercocks. 'Most unseemly,' he barked to Mama."

"And how did Mama reply?"

"She reminded him that friend Charles Somerford will be at the ball. . . ."

Lucinda shuddered. "I feared as much. Oh, Robert, whatever am I to do? I can never, ever marry such an odious man."

Robert took her hand. "You know I will help you in any way possible, Lucinda. Whenever you wish to confide in me, I am here, waiting."

She looked at him gratefully. "But you have problems of your own, Robert. Mama informs me that Papa is eager for you to begin studying books on estate management and animal husbandry."

Robert nodded gloomily. "I must confess, I awake each morning feeling as though a black cloud has settled above the bedcurtains and is waiting to envelop me." Then, after a moment, he brightened. "Let us not be downcast, sister. We are going to a ball! I appreciate that you will have to bear the presence of the dreadful Charles Somerford looming over you, but there will be music, and dancing—"

"Oh, yes!" exclaimed Lucinda, "I intend to enjoy myself, despite Mr. Charles Somerford!"

As was only to be expected, the Earl of Waverley's party travelled in style to the ball, in two carriages.

Lord Waverley, it was clear, was sorely wishing he was safely at home in his library, sipping his port. He glared from the carriage window as they swept up the drive of Brent Park, past a front lawn adorned with marble statues.

"What the deuce are they supposed to represent?" he demanded.

Lucinda hastened to explain. "Why, Papa, look, there is Mars, the god of war, and on the other side of the drive you can see Neptune, bearing his trident."

"I never heard such nonsense," snorted Lord Waverley. "I have never in my life seen such badly executed statues. Mars appears more like a common foot soldier than a god of war, and as for Neptune, stuck there on that miserable patch of grass instead of an ocean, and brandishing that pitchfork thing, why, to me he resembles no more than a lowly cart-filler."

Lucinda laughed and tucked her arm into her father's. "Now, Papa, do not be grumpy. I have no notion why you insist on feuding with Lady Falconbridge. She has always been most agreeable to me."

Lady Waverley sighed. "My lord does not approve of her ladyship riding to hounds, Lucinda."

"That is correct," nodded Lord Waverley. "A woman of her years should behave with dignity and decorum. Yet here she is, galloping around the countryside like a man, and then choosing to live in this ridiculous house with statues, and colonnades, and inconvenient flights of steps."

Lady Waverley patted his hand soothingly. She was aware that once he was settled in a comfortable seat within the ballroom, with a glass of good wine in his hand, Lord Waverley would thoroughly enjoy his evening.

He was simply a man who found pleasure in grousing. To admit that he was enjoying himself he would regard as a sign of weakness. And despite all his fears, the night was warm and still, enabling the Verney family to ascend the long flight of steps and enter the house in perfect style.

Lucinda felt a tremor of excitement tingling through her as she tied the ribbons on her velvet mask. From the ballroom came the tantalizing sounds of music and laughter. Oh, how wonderful it was to be at a ball! To be aware that for the next few hours she could give herself up to the exquisite pleasures of dancing and conversing with the many friends from the county she had not seen for months.

She gasped with delight as her party entered the ballroom. It resembled something from a fairytale, with the candlelit lusters shining like clusters of brilliant stars from the blue-painted ceiling . . . the marble columns entwined with gaily colored silk ribbons . . . and the perfumed revellers, their eyes behind their masks glittering as bright as the jewels that adorned their elegant ballgowns. And even the members of the band, playing at the end of the ballroom, were masked.

As Lord and Lady Waverley were so seldom seen in society, they were greeted with delight and soon found themselves the center of an animated party. Lucinda and her brothers and Melanie formed their own group in one of the silk-lined arbors that graced the ballroom.

Melanie quietly studied all the dancers and then commented to Lucinda, "You are by far the most beautiful girl in the room."

Lucinda flushed. Then, to her delight, the band struck up into the lilting rhythm of a new dance that was sweeping across Europe. "Oh, Robert, they are playing the waltz!"

She and Robert had often secretly practiced it together, in one of the quieter saloons of Waverley Hall.

"Come now, Lucinda, surely you do not wish to take the floor with your own brother," teased Robert. "How very tame!"

"But so few of the other people here are

familiar with the waltz," pleaded Lucinda. *Besides*, her eyes implored him, *at any moment Mr. Somerford will appear to claim his dances. Save me!*

"I cannot say I approve of this dance, Lucinda," said Frederick, frowning. "For once I agree with that poet fellow, Byron. He maintains that the waltz encourages wantonness. The minuet is a far more becoming dance for young ladies."

Robert grinned. "Tosh, brother. You are perfectly well aware that the only reason Byron disparages the waltz is that he has an injured foot which prevents him from dancing it successfully."

Melanie raised an inquiring eyebrow at her husband. "Why, Frederick, Lord Byron has a most disreputable reputation. I am surprised to learn that you are acquainted with *him.*"

Lucinda exchanged a smile with Robert as Frederick hastily explained, "Byron was a student at Harrow. I met him when we played cricket against his school. We are merely on nodding terms, Melanie, nothing more."

To Lucinda's relief, Robert took advantage of his brother's discomfiture to lead her onto the floor.

How especially lovely Lucinda looks when she dances, thought Melanie. The white silk of Lucinda's dress floated round her like a cloud, setting off to perfection her slim figure and translucent skin. The exertion of the dance brought a flush to her cheeks and a sparkle to the fine amethyst eyes, so that before long it was not only Melanie who was regarding the graceful golden-haired girl. All those in the ballroom, it seemed, were turning their heads to regard the brother and sister, and to remark that the lady Lucinda Verney had never looked so enchanting.

When the music stopped, there was an involuntary ripple of applause as Robert and Lucinda joined their family party. One person in the ballroom, however, did not applaud.

Charles Somerford bowed over Lucinda's hand and smiled icily down upon her. "If you are not too fatigued by all that whirling and twirling, the next dance is a minuet. May I have the pleasure? I find, do you not, that these more leisurely dances give one more opportunity to converse."

Frederick was nodding his approval, and a little way away, Lady Waverley smiled encouragement. Charles Somerford's fingers were like a vise on her hand as he led her back onto the dance floor.

"I believe," he said, as they moved forward, "that you owe me a certain explanation about a masked acquaintance of yours."

Lucinda inclined her head to smile politely at her hostess, Lady Falconbridge. Still apparently smiling, she said through gritted teeth, "I owe you nothing, Mr. Somerford. On the contrary, I am waiting for you to apologize for your coarse, vulgar, and unwarranted attack on me down by the river."

He laughed. The bruise on his chin, she noticed, had now dulled to a blotchy purplish brown. The sight of it gave her considerable satisfaction as he tightened his grip on her hand.

"Anyone who crosses me," he muttered softly, "lives to regret it." Unfortunately, the venom in his tone lost much of its effect as he stumbled and missed his step."

He was, thought Lucinda, the most appalling dancer. Ungainly, lumpish, and totally lacking in style.

Lucinda's tone was condescending. "I fear it is difficult to talk and dance at the same time, Mr. Somerford. Shall we concentrate on finishing this minuet without disgracing ourselves by falling over?"

He colored brick red. "We shall talk more at supper," he declared. "And it will be straight talking."

They finished the dance in silence. Then they returned to the arbor, and before he left her, Mr. Somerford commented, "Do not forget, Lady Lucinda, you are promised to me for the supper dance."

Again, thought Lucinda, it was a simple statement which her listening family would take purely at face value. But she knew that Charles Somerford was telling her: *You are engaged to me for the supper dance . . . and promised to me for life.*

Lucinda closed her eyes, so neither he nor her family would detect the loathing revealed there for him.

"Are you unwell?" inquired Melanie. "You are suddenly very pale."

Lucinda smiled wanly. "It is merely the

exertion of the dance, Melanie. I shall step outside and breathe the fresh air."

Melanie, who had been about to dance with her husband, said kindly, "Let me accompany you."

"No, you enjoy the cotillion," insisted Lucinda. "I shall only be a moment."

Leaving the ballroom, she wandered through the lofty halls and saloons until she reached a large oak door. Pushing it open, she breathed a welcome draft of cool evening air. She stepped outside and found to her delight that she was in a flagged courtyard. In the center gushed a small fountain, the sprays of water shimmering like diamonds in the light of the moon. Enchanted, Lucinda sat down on the fountain edge, revelling in the refreshing droplets of moisture misting her hair and bare arms.

From the ballroom came the strains of another waltz. And soon, Lucinda realized miserably, there would be the supper dance, which was promised to Charles Somerford. She gazed dejectedly into the pool, reluctant to return and face a proposal from Charles Somerford after supper. In fact, she decided, it would be just like Mr. Somerford to choose to propose *before* supper, so that with the business successfully concluded, he could digest his meal in peace.

Immersed in her thoughts, Lucinda did not hear the footsteps of the man crossing the courtyard. The man who all evening had watched her every word and smile and move. The man who had come now to claim her.

FIVE

His strong hands encircled her waist, whirling her around and into his arms. Breathless with shock, Lucinda was powerless to cry out, or protest.

And then he laughed, softly.

Such a distinctive, amused, dearly familiar laugh. As she melted into his arms and allowed him to guide her into the slow, graceful movement of the waltz, Lucinda realized that, of course, in her heart of hearts, she had been hoping . . . expecting that Miles would be mingling with the revellers at Brent Park. A masked ball was, after all, the most perfect cover for her gentleman of the night.

Now I know, she thought exultantly, as he led her expertly around the shimmering fountain, why I felt so excited tonight. It was not merely the anticipation of the dancing and the music. No, deep down I was expecting *him* to be here.

And he had not disappointed her.

They spoke not a word, the dark-haired man and the golden-haired girl, as they danced together in the deserted courtyard. What words were needed? The strains of the music floating out into the scented, April night . . . the perfect rhythm of their steps . . . the touch of hand on hand . . . all expressed far more than mere speech could ever do.

All too soon, the music faded away. The waltz was over. Miles executed a most elegant bow, and Lucinda swept him a courtly curtsey in return.

"Lady Lucinda! I say, Lady Lucinda . . . are you out here?"

Lucinda's blood ran cold. "It is Charles Somerford. He has come looking for me, to claim the supper dance!"

Swiftly, Miles drew her into a shadowed corner of the courtyard. Just in time. A second later, the oak door opened, and Mr. Somerford strode angrily out into the night. Lucinda had difficulty restraining the impulse to laugh as the moonlight illuminated Charles Somerford's livid face. Clearly, he was beside himself with fury at her for causing him all this bother, inconvenience, and embarrassment. She noticed Miles's broad shoulders were trembling and realized that he, too, was deriving no little amusement from her beau's discomfiture.

"Lady Lucinda?" called Charles Somerford again. Then he muttered to himself, "No, dash it, the minx is not out here. Snatch me! I have never known a woman play cat and mouse like this one. But so help me, I'll make her mine in the end. And then she'll learn who's master!"

He returned to the house, slamming the door behind him.

Lucinda let out a deep breath. "Heavens, now what am I to do? If I return now to the ballroom, I can imagine Mr. Somerford reprimanding me in one breath for avoiding him and then proceeding straight with the next to inform me that he is prepared to overlook my misdemeanors and do me the honor of making me his wife!"

Miles laughed, the gray eyes beneath the mask glinting like steel in the moonlight. "Clearly, you will not be safe with Mr. Somerford. So I believe the best solution would be for me to abduct you. Just for an hour, you understand."

Lucinda stared up at him, her heart racing. "Abduct? Whatever do you mean?"

"I intend to take you on a watery journey," he said, "and show you an enchanted island by the silvered light of the moon. Now," he continued briskly, "are you prepared to be abducted without fuss, or must I pick you up in my arms and carry you off by force?"

"Oh, but you are outrageous!" laughed Lucinda. Never in her life had she felt so happy, so carefree. Entering into the spirit of the ad-

93

venture, she struck a dramatic pose and declaimed, "Take me where you will, sir. I am a poor defenseless woman, too weak to resist!"

"Not too weak to run a little way, I trust," said Miles drily. "I *could* carry you all the way down to the lake, but it would impede our progress somewhat."

He took her hand, and they slipped from the courtyard by a side gate. They ran through a glade of aspen trees, and there beyond lay the calm waters of the Brent Park lake. A boat was moored by the water's edge, and within minutes Lucinda was seated inside it, with Miles rowing powerfully toward the small central island.

Trailing a hand in the cool, inky water, Lucinda threw back her head as the gentle April breeze ruffled her golden tresses. Behind her, she could hear the distant sound of music and laughter from Brent Park house. She imagined Charles Somerford, raging from room to room in his search for her. Eventually, she supposed, he would inform her parents that she was missing. There would be the most appalling hue and cry.

But I care not! thought Lucinda. Let them say their fill, and punish me as they will. Nothing matters except this one precious hour with my gallant masked friend.

Miles was smiling at her. "Lucinda, your eyes are shining brighter than the stars. What are you thinking?"

She spread her delicate hands. "Just that I shall have to face the most dreadful interrogation when I return to the ball—and that I do not give a spangle for any of it! Somehow, here with you, I feel so free and wonderful. My father will probably lock me in my room with nothing but bread and water. But I do not care. I shall have the memory of this hour to sustain me."

She stopped, suddenly horrified at what she had said. Never in her life had she spoken in such an outright fashion to anyone except her brother Robert. Yet intuitively, with Miles, she felt she could say anything and not be misunderstood.

His voice was deep and tender as he replied, "You are a brave, spirited girl, Lucinda. I admire you enormously. You must not worry about what your parents will say to you later. I believe that in everyone's life there are certain rare occasions when we are in some magical way protected from harm, reprisals, and recriminations. This is one of those times, Lucinda. I give you my word, you will come to no harm either now with me, or later when you return to the ball."

She believed him. She knew nothing about him, except that his name was Miles, and he was clearly a gentleman. She had never seen his face unmasked. She knew nothing of his past, his family, or why he chose to cloak himself and his identity in secrecy.

All she knew, with a joyous certainty, was that he would never deceive her. He had said, on the occasion of their first meeting, that he was her friend. And wherever he led her tonight, or any other night, she would put her trust in him and follow.

When they neared the island, Miles eased the boat through the reeded shallows, tied it to a tree stump, and assisted Lucinda onto the mossy bank.

"Come," he said, taking her hand and leading her along the path, until they reached a secluded inlet where three willow trees dipped graceful curtseys into the water.

On the far side of the lake twinkled the lights of Brent Park, which prompted her to inquire, "How came you to gain admittance to the ball, Miles? Why, even my father was obliged to show the steward his invitation card. He was most aggrieved, and stamped off immediately to have words with Lady Falconbridge on the matter."

Miles smiled. "My life has been unconventional, Lucinda. In particular, I was privileged to enjoy an education which not only equipped me to speak in four languages, to duel, to shoot and ride with equal dexterity . . . but just as valuable was the lesson in the art of slipping quietly in and out of other people's houses."

Intrigued, Lucinda remarked, "I wish you would tell me more about yourself. I am beginning to suspect you to be a thorough rogue—a gentleman highwayman. My brother Robert told me of one such who stopped a coach and dared to dance a quadrille with a lady before divesting her of her pearls!"

"Regrettably," laughed Miles, "I have not the time to spare for such pleasant dalliance. It is impossible to tell you more, Lucinda, but believe me, there is a serious purpose behind my wearing of the mask. A deadly serious purpose."

Something in his tone sent a shiver down Lucinda's spine. Toward her, Miles had been unfailingly gallant. Yet now she realized that he was indeed a man of steel, who when the occasion demanded could be utterly ruthless.

He took her hand and said gravely, "We have a common bond, Lucinda, you and I."

"We have?" she whispered.

"You are a lovely young girl, the prized daughter of a titled family, convinced you are doomed to marry a man you loathe. Whilst I am forced to travel in the shadows, until the mission I have set myself is completed. In different ways, Lucinda, you and I are victims of the conventions of life."

She nodded, a glimmering of understanding beginning to dawn.

Miles went on, "But now, just for one hour, we have been given the opportunity to steal a march on our fates. This is our enchanted night, Lucinda. It is time out of time, a special gift of a magic hour which exists purely for our delight."

She gazed up at him, breathless. By the light of the moon his hair shone blue-black. Behind the velvet mask his gray eyes held her completely in thrall.

"Do you recollect," he murmured, "when we stood under some other willow trees in the sunshine, and I told you that at some time in the future I would teach you how to kiss?"

"I remember," Lucinda whispered, her heart beating wildly.

"The time has come," declared the man in the mask.

In the space of a few short seconds a myriad of thoughts and impressions flashed through Lucinda's mind. Her mother's horror, her father's wrath if they could but see her now . . . alone on this lakeland island with a man they would undoubtedly brand as a common rogue, a blackguard . . . then Charles Somerford, the man she was doomed to marry . . . the coarse face, menacing eyes, and fleshy lips . . . if her father insisted, she would be condemned to share her life, her bed, with a man she loathed and detested.

And then she looked upon Miles, standing tall and strong before her. His hands rested lightly upon her shoulders, but he had made no further move toward her.

"Fear not," he said, as if reading her mind. "I shall not force you, Lucinda. The decision is yours."

As she gazed into his rugged, handsome face, Lucinda knew what her answer would be. It is wrong, and shameful, she thought, but I care not! If I am to spend the rest of my life in misery with a man I despise—a man who makes my flesh creep when he so much as touches my hand—then yes, I will grasp this chance, this one chance of happiness with Miles. He is right, this is a rare, enchanted time out of time.

Shyly, she raised a trembling hand and pressed it over the firm, long fingers that rested on her shoulder. "Miles," she murmured.

He understood. Masterfully, he swept her into his arms. Then his hands caressed her silken hair, tilting back her head. Lucinda closed her eyes as his lips found hers with a sweet, tender authority that kindled within her a flame of passionate longing. Oh, how willingly she surrendered to the demands of his embrace!

After a long time he released her and held her close to him, her head resting against his broad chest.

"I have wanted you so much," he whispered. "You were not aware, but earlier at the ball, I was watching while you waltzed with a tall, fair-haired young man."

"My brother Robert," Lucinda breathed.

"You looked so delightful," said Miles, "with your gossamer white dress, and your golden hair haloed in the candlelight. It was all I could do to prevent myself rushing onto the dance floor and taking you into my arms there and then."

Lucinda smiled, imagining the consternation such an act would have caused!

"I must take you back now," Miles said. "I fear our enchanted hour is almost at an end, my lovely one."

Lucinda let out a long, shuddering sigh. "Yes, it is over. And I must prepare to face the music!"

"Fear not," said Miles reassuringly. "I am your friend, remember? Do you think I would allow you to walk into danger or difficulty? I promise you that no harm, not so much as a single reproach, will come your way because of your adventure with me."

As he spoke, he guided her back along the

path toward the moored roving boat. They travelled back across the lake in silence, except for the soft dipping of the oars in the water. Then Miles escorted her up the bank, through the glade of aspen trees, to the side door that led back to the courtyard.

"I must leave you here," he said.

She gazed up at him. A dim light from the house was shining onto his face, and she tried to etch his features onto her memory. For who knew where—or when—she would see him again?

Once more, Miles demonstrated his uncanny ability to read her mind.

"I have many urgent affairs to attend to, Lucinda. But rest assured, you will be ever in my thoughts. And if you should need me, you will find me at the Blue Boar Inn, on the Guildford road."

Lucinda flushed with happiness. By telling her this much, he had proved that he trusted her. He was indeed her friend, and her protector. She wondered if he would take her into his arms and kiss her farewell.

But this was not to be. Gently, Miles raised her hand and brushed it lightly with his lips. He then guided her through the side door and closed it behind her. Once more she was alone in the courtyard where the fountain played.

Lucinda longed to linger here awhile, and relive her magic hour with Miles . . . retracing every minute from the moment he had swept her into his arms and waltzed her round the fountain.

But her parents and Charles Somerford were waiting. Reluctantly, Lucinda reentered the house, deposited her cloak in the ladies' dressing room, and hurried back to the ballroom.

Perhaps, she thought, surveying the laughing, dancing revellers, I have not been missed at all! It could be that I was observed leaving the ballroom and Mr. Somerford and my parents assumed I was feeling fatigued, so had retired to one of the saloons to rest.

"Lucinda!" Lady Waverley's sharp tone shredded all Lucinda's hopes. "Wherever have you been, child? And my, just look at your dress!"

Horrified, Lucinda stared down at the hem of her white silk dress. It was three inches deep in mud.

"And your slippers, too!" exclaimed the Countess indignantly. "Why, they are thoroughly soiled. Quite ruined!"

Lucinda searched for words. They would not come.

"Thank heaven," Lady Waverley ran on, "that your father has retired to the smoking room and is not present to witness your disgrace."

Charles Somerford, who was escorting the Countess at that moment, said meaningfully, "Lady Waverley and I have been most concerned about you, Lady Lucinda."

"It is most vexing and most rude of you to disappear when you had promised the supper dance to Mr. Somerford. Kindly explain yourself."

Lucinda swallowed. A thousand improbable excuses flashed through her mind, only to be rejected as totally unbelievable. "I . . . I can explain, Mama. You see, well, the fact is, I—"

And then, miraculously, came the sound of Melanie's sweet voice behind her, declaring calmly, "Oh, Lucinda, how dreadful of me to have caused you so much trouble."

Lucinda whirled around. Melanie took her by the arm and said to Lady Waverley, "I must own that it is all my fault. I was feeling a little faint, and Lucinda kindly offered to fetch my smelling bottle which I had foolishly left in the carriage."

Charles Somerford said smoothly, "But surely, my dear Lady Alford, it would have been more in order for one of the footmen to have fetched your smelling bottle."

Melanie's soft brown eyes regarded him guilelessly. "Oh, Mr. Somerford, you know how confusing it is in the coachyard, with so many carriages pitched in together. The poor footman would have taken an hour identifying our carriage, and by that time I should have found myself in a dead swoon from the heat. I retired to one of the saloons, and Lucinda sweetly volunteered to go to the courtyard herself."

Lady Waverley looked mollified. "That was very kind of you, Lucinda. But I am surprised at Lady Falconbridge, allowing her coachyard to swim in mud."

"I lost my way in the dark coming back," said Lucinda quickly. "One of the grooms had left a pail of dirty water. Foolishly, I kicked it over, so muddying my dress and slippers."

Lady Waverley seemed totally convinced, but Lucinda's inward sigh of relief was curtailed as Mr. Somerford said keenly, "Yet it seems, Lady Lucinda, that your errand was in vain. You do not appear to be carrying the smelling bottle."

Before Lucinda could attempt a reply, Melanie said, with a rueful flutter of her hands. "Now, Mr. Somerford, you seem determined to put me to the blush! I had forgotten that I left the smelling bottle in the ladies' dressing room. It is most ungallant of you to reveal that I sent poor Lucinda on a completely fruitless errand."

Charles Somerford was silenced. But his pale blue eyes spoke volumes to Lucinda. He did not believe Melanie's story. Yet he had no way of disproving it.

Instead, he said to Lucinda, "Unfortunately, the ball is now drawing to a close. It will soon be time for us all to unmask. But I should like the honor of having the last dance with you, Lady Lucinda."

Lucinda gazed into his coarse, loathsome face. And suddenly, his visage faded, and instead it was as if she was looking at Miles. She remembered the expression in the eyes of her masked friend and protector just before he kissed her. She recalled all the tender passion of that kiss. And she knew, in that instant, that she loved Miles. That whoever he was, whatever his reasons for living in the shadows, she would always love him.

She heard Charles Somerford cough discreetly.

Lady Waverley said, in a slightly embarrassed tone, "Lucinda, perhaps you did not hear? Mr. Somerford has asked you to honor him with the last dance."

Lucinda flashed him a radiant smile. "Of course, Mr. Somerford. I should be delighted."

Kicking off her slippers, she allowed him to take her hand. Once again, all eyes were on Lucinda as she and her partner took their places in the cotillion.

Why, went the buzz of speculation round the ballroom, Lucinda Verney looks totally enamoured with Charles Somerford. And indeed, such was the radiance of her expression that no one even noticed she was dancing in stockinged feet.

"I do believe," Lady Waverley commented to her son Frederick, "that Lucinda has had a change of heart. Just look at her! She has the glowing eyes and soft smile of a girl truly in love."

No one so much as suspected that while Lucinda smiled and made her graceful way through the cotillion, she was thinking of Miles . . . their time on the island . . . his kiss . . . and how much she loved him.

No one suspected, that is, except her dark-eyed sister-in-law, Melanie.

Lucinda awoke to the sound of rain gently pattering on her windowpane. Yet she felt so joyful, it was as if the chamber was flooded with sunshine. Lying in her cozy, curtained bed, listening to the familiar early morning sounds of the house—the shouts of the stableboys, the screech of the peacocks strutting on the lawn,

Robert and Frederick on the terrace below, still bickering about that hunter—Lucinda found it hard to believe that last night she had been caught up in such an enthralling adventure.

But it had all really happened. The enchanted hour on the island was hers to treasure forever. Whatever befell her in the future, she would have that golden memory to console her.

And Miles had kissed her! Lucinda's face burned against the cool pillowcase. What tender passion had there been between them! Never in her wildest dreams had she imagined herself to be capable of such emotion. I should be ashamed, she thought, abandoning myself so willfully to his embrace.

But it was right! I know it! And I shall never regret that kiss. Never.

Slipping from the bed, she cleansed herself in the warm water her maid had brought in earlier. When she had dressed in her white muslin gown, she noticed that the maid had not yet removed the soiled dancing slippers.

Melanie! thought Lucinda as the later events of last night came flooding back. I must speak to Melanie.

She glanced out of the window and saw that the rain had been no more than an April shower. Already the skies were clearing, leaving the lawns and gardens below bathed in morning sunshine. As Lucinda watched, Melanie herself appeared on the lawn. She was carrying a basket and scissors and was quietly engaged in snipping off spring flowers to take into the house.

Lucinda ran lightly down the back stairs

of the house and slipped out of the garden door.

"Melanie!" she called. "I must speak with you."

Melanie smiled and bent to cut some dancing yellow daffodils. "Good morning, sister. I trust you slept well after the excitement of the ball?"

Lucinda took her arm. "I must thank you for coming to my assistance last night."

"Are not these daffodils beautiful?" inquired Melanie, touching their vivid petals. "They look so English, it seems impossible to believe that they were originally a Spanish flower."

"Yes, they are lovely," replied Lucinda impatiently, "But Melanie, tell me how you knew—"

"I declare, there is nothing more delightful," went on Melanie serenely, "than an English garden after the rain. Take a deep breath, sister. Does it not smell sweet?"

"Melanie," pleaded Lucinda, "I think I shall die if you do not tell me why you came to my aid last night."

"Are you not reading too much into the situation?" murmured Melanie. "I perceived that you were in some difficulty and made up what I hoped was a convincing story to save you. It was a sisterly act, nothing more."

Melanie's soft brown eyes looked so innocent. Yet some sixth sense urged Lucinda to ask, "Miles asked you to help me, did he not?"

Melanie looked hastily away. But not before Lucinda had observed a telltale flicker in her eyes. "I love him," Lucinda said quietly. "I must know more about him. Please tell me all you know. For I am sure you do know more than I."

Lucinda saw her cast a guarded glance around the garden. But they were quite alone, apart from the birds singing in the trees.

"Very well," said Melanie gravely, "I will tell you what I know, though most like it will not be enough totally to satisfy your curiosity. Some weeks ago, returning from the circulating library, I was unfortunate enough to stumble and turn my ankle. A gentleman noticed my plight and most kindly transported me home on his horse."

"Miles," breathed Lucinda.

"Yes," nodded Melanie. "On arrival at Curzon Street, I saw to my dismay that Frederick had unexpectedly returned a few minutes ahead of me."

"And you were in possession of romances from the circulating library!"

"I was carrying them in a small net bag," said Melanie, her face paling at the memory. "As Miles assisted me from the horse, I pushed the bag into his hands, murmured my thanks, and hobbled as speedily as I could into the house. Fortunately, he seemed not at all put out by my strange behavior. Then the following day, while my husband was out, a messenger returned my books, with a note which said, *Secrecy is the very essence of Romance—Miles.*"

Lucinda smiled. "He had understood, then, that you dared not allow your husband to see you reading those novels. But did you know that Miles would be present at the masked ball?"

"That I did not," said Melanie. "But while you were dancing with Robert, I noticed this gentleman standing a little apart from everyone else, and his eyes were fixed on you. His noble bearing convinced me that it was Miles, though what he was doing at Lady Falconbridge's ball I could not imagine. He must have sensed that my eyes were upon him, for he glanced across at me and bowed. I was not sure that he had recognized me in my mask, but a little later he passed by and pressed a note into my hand. It begged me to explain your absence in a little while. So that is just what I did."

Lucinda clasped her hands. "Oh, I wish I knew more about him. It is so tantalizing knowing so little!"

Melanie laughed sympathetically. "But will you not now tell me how you chanced to meet Miles? And what there is between you? I have been most intrigued about your situation."

"Melanie, how thoughtless of me. Of course I will tell you everything. But—"

"Fear not," smiled Melanie, "It shall be our secret."

So as they strolled amongst the forget-me-knots clouding the path, Lucinda told Melanie about her meetings with her gallant masked friend.

"How romantic!" breathed Melanie.

"But now we are torn apart once more," sighed Lucinda, "and I know not when, if ever, we may meet again."

Melanie said thoughtfully, "From what you

have told me of Miles, I would judge him to be an extremely determined man. If he decides that you shall meet, then nothing will keep him from you." She pressed Lucinda's hand. "As you know, Frederick and I are returning to London today. But rest assured, sister, that if it is within my power, I shall do everything I can to help you."

"I am grateful to you," murmured Lucinda, "but I believe my more immediate need is for a miracle."

Cantering toward Waverley Hall was Lady Falconbridge, accompanied by a grim-faced Charles Somerford. And Lucinda had no doubt in her mind that the purpose of his visit was to ask her father for her hand in marriage.

SIX

Lady Falconbridge strode into the morning room. In her customary brisk fashion she threw her gloves and riding crop down onto the table, smudging the dinner menu which Lady Waverley had just painstakingly copied out for Cook.

"Good day, Lady Waverley. I brought Mr. Somerford along with me, as he desired to have a word with your good lord before he returns to London this morning."

Lucinda and Melanie exchanged glances. So Mr. Somerford was quitting Surrey! Lucinda hardly dared hope. . . .

Lady Waverly rose to her feet, looking fussed. "Dear me. You know how Lord Waverly hates being interrupted at his breakfast. And it was devilled kidneys this morning, too. His favorite."

"Couldn't be helped," barked Lady Falconbridge. "Mr. Somerford was most insistent on seeking an interview here this morning. Anyway, it doesn't do to allow these men to become too set in their ways. It's bracing for Lord Waverley to have his breakfast routine upset now and then. They have both now gone off to the library."

"But the fire will not be lit in there yet!" exclaimed Lady Waverley, hastening toward the bellcord. "I must call for a housemaid—"

Lady Falconbridge stayed her hand. "Diddle-daddle! They are two grown men, not babies. They'll survive in that stuffy library of yours for half an hour without a fire."

Melanie swiftly changed the subject. "See what pretty spring flowers I cut for you, ma'am. Shall I arrange them for you? They would look delightful on your writing table."

"How thoughtful of you," said Lady Waverley, smiling. "It has been such a joy having you here, Melanie. I shall miss you dreadfully. As, no doubt, will Lucinda."

Lady Falconbridge was growing restive in the face of all these pleasantries. Suddenly, she interrupted. "I hear Lord Alford turned down that hunter the other day?"

Lucinda nodded. "He was suspicious because it had recently been exercised. Frederick feared the horse might be slightly lame."

"That husband of yours is too cautious for words," Lady Falconbridge informed Melanie. "You ought to shake him up a bit. Otherwise, he'll turn out just like his father—a tedious traditionalist who quakes at the thought of setting foot outside his own estate."

"Really, Lady Falconbridge," said the Countess coolly, "I cannot allow you to criticize my lord in that manner. He has been a good husband and provider. What more can a woman ask?"

"I am merely recommending that Lady Alford keep a lively mind and spirit about her. You never know—in time, some of it may rub off on Frederick."

Lucinda hid a smile as she observed her sister calmly arranging the daffodils in a vase. There was no cause for anyone to offer Melanie advice, Lucinda reflected. Beneath that quiet, modest exterior, Melanie was most certainly a girl of rare spirit and initiative.

Lucinda was sincerely sorry that she and Frederick were returning to London today. Already, she and Melanie had become firm friends, but Lucinda was convinced there was still more to learn about the soft-eyed girl her brother had married. When Melanie departed this morning, Lucinda knew she would have lost a valuable ally.

Of course, there was always her brother Robert. A part of her longed to tell him all about Miles. But Robert was a man. Although they had shared many childhood adventures, Lucinda felt that Robert might not approve of her escapades with Miles. Was it really the proper behavior for his *sister?*

Then again, in past years, Robert had invariably been the leader. It had been he who had dreamed up those wild schemes for riding on steam trains, or learning to waltz, and teaching her to ride bareback.

Lucinda smiled, recalling the day Robert had come across his eight-year-old sister making a bride's bouquet from a bunch of cow parsley. Robert had scoffed that she was playing prissy games and showed her instead how to make an effective pea-shooter from the cow parsley.

They had fired missiles at the local doctor as he rode past, knocking off the poor gentleman's hat. Fortunately, Dr. Webster had a sense of humor and refrained from reporting the incident to Lord Waverley, thus saving Robert a thrashing and Lucinda a day locked in her room with bread and water.

But how would Robert react, Lucinda mused, if he learned that she was now acting on her own initiative? Already, he was suspicious of that incident by the river, when she had alleged that Mr. Somerford had tripped and injured his jaw.

If Robert knew of her involvement with Miles, would he then insist on masterminding the adventure himself? Yes, Lucinda was convinced he would persist in tracking Miles down and discovering once and for all who he was and why he behaved in such an antisocial manner. Surely, Robert would refuse to rest until he had solved the mystery.

And that I cannot allow him to do, Lucinda decided. Miles has shown his trust in me. Clearly, he is involved in some private mission that he alone can determine. For Robert to interfere would be impudent and untimely. And for me to permit such meddling would be a betrayal of the trust Miles has placed in me.

Apart from which, Lucinda knew that Robert had problems of his own. He had still not abandoned his scheme of joining the Army. But Lord Waverley was adamant that his younger son must stay at Waverley and learn the intricacies of estate management.

When the Earl entered the morning room, all four ladies looked at him expectantly.

"Mr. Somerford has departed for London," he declared, seating himself in his favorite chair near the window. "He asked me to apologize for not taking his leave of you all, but I gather he has important business to attend to."

Lady Waverley asked the question that was uppermost in everyone's mind. "And may I inquire, my lord, why he desired to talk with you so urgently?"

"Mr. Somerford will shortly be returning to Surrey," announced his lordship. "And from our conversation this morning, I am confident that he will then make a formal offer of marriage for our daughter Lucinda."

The Countess clapped her hands with delight and triumph. "There, Lucinda! What did I tell you?"

Lucinda was stooping to pick up a fallen daffodil, and no one could see her face.

Lady Falconbridge said keenly, "Well, girl! Do you nurture any feelings of affection for Mr. Somerford?"

"I have known him so little time," replied Lucinda primly. "I fear my affections are not that speedily engaged."

"Then you would be well advised to put your skates on," declared her father. "You will never receive a better offer."

"Don't harass the girl," boomed Lady Falconbridge. "She is quite correct—love needs time to bloom. After all, my own Percy courted me for three years. There was not an inch of Surrey we did not ride across together, and every step of the way he showered me with the most extravagant compliments. It was unbelievably romantic."

Even Melanie could not repress a stare of amazement at this astounding revelation.

"All right," said Lady Falconbridge, "I appreciate that it sounds incredible now. You all regard me as an eccentric old woman. And maybe I am. But I was young once, and I know the virtue of taking your time in selecting your partner. Percy and I were sublimely happy."

"Of course you were," said Lady Waverley soothingly, "and naturally, we are eager for Lucinda to be content in her marriage, too. But it is a fact that Mr. Somerford seems a most eligible gentleman. Surely she could soon learn to love someone with his income *and* the prospect of a Dukedom?"

Lord Waverley nodded. "That is why he was compelled to hasten back to London, for an important meeting with his lawyers about the business of proving he is the rightful heir to the dukedom."

Lucinda was burning to know more about this, but at the same time she was resolved to utter no word of interest in Mr. Somerford or his future prospects.

But Melanie understood, and was able to pose the question for her: "I do not understand, my lord. Surely it is a clear-cut matter. Either Mr. Somerford is, or is not, the heir?"

Lord Waverley patted her hand. "It is more complicated than that, my dear. You see, as I understand the matter from Mr. Somerford, the old Duke of Lexburgh had one son, who was of course his heir. When the old Duke died, the title naturally passed to the son. But only a month afterward, the son was discovered tragically drowned."

"How dreadful," breathed Melanie.

"Save your sympathy," snapped Lady Falconbridge. "The Lexburghs were a totally disreputable bunch. The old Duke womanized, and his son gambled. Why, the stories I could tell you—"

"The old Duke," interrupted Lord Waverley loudly, "had two brothers. The younger one, Matthew, died some years ago and was Mr. Somerford's father. But the middle brother, Darcy, was something of a wayward character. He disappeared off into the blue when he was in his early twenties. Travelled across to Italy or some such foreign place, and has not been heard of since."

Lady Falconbridge drummed her fingers on the writing table. "I see. So if they can locate the missing brother Darcy, then he will become the Duke of Lexburgh. Otherwise, the title passes to Charles Somerford, the younger brother's son?"

"Precisely," said Lord Waverley. "Mr. Somerford is quite confident that his Uncle Darcy is dead. The lawyers are 'making great harvest of a little corn,' he declares, in mounting this huge search for him."

"But it would seem," said Melanie, once again asking what Lucinda wanted to know, "that the inquiries are going to take some little time yet?"

"Indeed yes," nodded Lord Waverley, who to Lucinda's ears was beginning to sound more like the hateful Mr. Somerford every minute. "After all, it is by no means certain that Darcy did in fact settle in Italy. He could be situated anywhere in Europe."

"Or even the New World," murmured Lucinda hopefully.

Lord Waverley looked at her sharply. "Wherever he is, Mr. Somerford is confident that the lawyers will soon receive intelligence of his demise. Then Mr. Somerford, as Duke of Lexburgh, intends to move immediately into Lexburgh Castle. Naturally, he will need a wife beside him."

Fortunately, Lucinda's attempt at a reply was curtailed by the arrival of Frederick to announce that the luggage was being loaded onto the carriage and he desired Melanie to be ready to depart in precisely fifteen minutes.

The entire family, and Lady Falconbridge, gathered on the front steps of Waverley Hall to bid Lord and Lady Alford farewell.

Before Melanie entered the carriage, she kissed Lucinda and whispered, "Courage, sister. And remember, I shall do everything in my power to help you."

Nevertheless as Lucinda watched the coach disappear out of sight down the drive, she felt a wave of sadness sweep over her. For with Melanie's departure, she felt she had lost her one last precious link with Miles.

Try as she might, Lucinda could not shake off her feeling of listlessness. She occupied herself with embroidery, beadwork, and the delicate water colors she executed so exquisitely.

Yet all the time her heart was heavy. The weather, too, seemed to turn with her mood. There were few sunny, springlike days. Instead, the rain either fell in depressing gray sheets or misted the gentle Surrey hills in a fine drizzle.

Lady Waverley, recalling Lucinda's radiant expression during her last dance with Charles Somerford at the masked ball, completely mistook the reason for her daughter's low spirits.

"Be patient, my dear," she said coming across Lucinda in the music room, playing a sad, haunting tune on the pianoforte, "Mr. Somerford will soon be back in Surrey. You have not much longer to wait."

Lucinda's fingers froze, striking a discordant note on the keys.

The Countess went on, "I understand how reluctant you are to admit to your father your growing affection for Mr. Somerford. These things do take time. Lady Falconbridge is quite right. It is just one of the tiresome ways of the world, I am afraid, that the menfolk concern themselves with your beau's property and income—in order to have you properly settled—whereas to us women, there is the matter of the heart to be considered, as well."

"Yes, Mama," Lucinda agreed, her hands sweeping across the ivories.

But I have already given my heart, she thought, as the music swelled to a glorious crescendo. A masked man took me into his arms by the lake and kissed me. Oh, how tenderly he kissed me! And I fell hopelessly, irrevocably, in love with him.

It was only later, as Lucinda sat in the windowseat of her chamber, gazing out at the rain, that it occurred to her to wonder what Miles's feelings were for her. She loved him, of that she was convinced. But what was she to him? He had never told her he loved her. Even when he kissed her, not a word of love had he uttered.

Was it, then, no more than an amusing escapade for him? Did he merely seek to pass an entertaining hour, spiriting me away to the island, to take advantage of my thirst for adventure and romance?

No! I will not regard him thus, Lucinda vowed. He is a gentleman. He would never seek merely to trifle with me. I will not think of it.

In an endeavor to blot such disagreeable reflections from her mind, she took up a new novel which Melanie had kindly left for her. It was entitled: *The Female Soldier; or, The Surprising Life and Adventures of Hannah Snell.*

Lucinda settled down to read, and within minutes was totally absorbed. So much so, that she was late dressing for dinner and very nearly incurred her father's wrath by arriving at the dining table only just ahead of the soup.

After dinner, Lord Waverley retired to the library and Lady Waverley went early to bed, leaving Robert and his sister alone in the drawing room.

Robert sprawled on the sofa while Lucinda poured the tea.

How tired he looks, she thought, observing the shadows beneath his blue eyes. Robert's education in estate management had now begun in earnest. To give him his due, Robert really was making a determined effort to get to grips with the subject he detested. Every day, even in the most blinding rain, he had been out riding around the estate, visiting farms, talking to the tenants, and listening to his father explaining how things should be run.

More than that, Robert had started studying on his own, rising an hour earlier than usual to pore over books on animal husbandry and other related subjects.

No wonder he looks fatigued, mused Lucinda as she handed him his tea. "How was it today, brother?" she inquired sympathetically.

Robert stretched out his long legs. "Just as bad as usual. The deuce of it is that Papa says, on the one hand, that I am to learn all about the estate, but when I make a suggestion, he shouts me down and tells me not to interfere!"

Lucinda smiled. She could well imagine the scene! "That is Papa's way, I am afraid, Robert."

"The whole endeavor is a mistake," declared Robert. "No land should have two masters, especially when they disagree as much as Papa and I. I appreciate that I have to learn, and I am trying. But my father is so entrenched in the old methods, he will not consider anything new."

"What innovations had you in mind?" asked Lucinda, nibbling at a candied violet.

Robert leaned forward, his hands clenched together. "For a start, Papa has no notion of the first principles of crop rotation."

"Neither, I must confess, have I," said Lucinda faintly.

Robert smiled. "It simply means that you do not grow the same crop on the same piece of land year after year. You grow wheat one year, swede the next, then barley, and then clover. In this way, the soil is not drained of its goodness."

"I see," nodded Lucinda, rather impressed by Robert's knowledge. "What other ideas have you?"

"Well," said Robert, warming to his theme and pleased by Lucinda's interest, "you've heard Papa complain time and time again about the sandy soil on the estate?"

"Papa says it is too light and will not retain moisture, especially in a hot, dry summer. Not," Lucinda commented wryly, glancing out at the driving rain, "that drought seems likely to be a problem this year."

"Oh, the weather will clear, you'll see," said Robert. "But Papa's method has always been to grow broom. After two years, it is cut and dug into the soil, to bulk it up. Yet as I told my father this morning, that is a very expensive way of dealing with the problem."

"Because while the land is taken up with acres of broom, there is no room to grow a more productive crop?" suggested Lucinda.

"That is exactly right!" exclaimed Robert.

"But what else can be used instead of the broom?" mused Lucinda, her lively curiosity aroused by the subject.

"The latest remedy for dry soil is something called marl," explained Robert. "It is a mixture of clay and carbonate of lime, which has been used very successfully in other parts of the country. You simply dig the mixture in, and then the crops can be planted immediately. But will Papa agree? Oh no! He says his father, and his father before him, used the old methods very successfully. Why should he change?"

Listening to Robert, Lucinda could see very well both sides of the thorny situation. She saw her father, set in his traditional ways (which, after all, had served him well all his life) and now endeavoring to train his son.

But instead of nodding respectfully, and agreeing with everything his father said, Lord Waverley's headstrong son had the temerity to make suggestions and demand change. *Change!* The very word was anathema to the Earl.

It was a complete clash of personalities, reflected Lucinda. How could father and son ever agree, when their temperaments differed so greatly? It was hardly surprising that Robert was eager to adopt new methods. All his life he had loved to be first with anything new.

Lucinda sympathized, but could see no immediate answer to the problem. Clearly, two grown men could not live together successfully under one roof. It was time for Robert to spread his wings and leave the nest. But Lord Waverley had decreed that *that* was not to be.

Robert arose and paced restlessly up and down the room. "Dash it all, Lucinda! I feel so . . . so *caged!*"

Lucinda cast desperately around in her mind for something to divert and entertain him. "If you promise not to tell Papa," she said, "I will lend you the most fascinating book I have been reading. It is all about an enterprising woman called Hannah Snell, who ran away to join the Army!"

"You mean she disguised herself as a man?" asked Robert.

"She did indeed. What is more, she served in not only the Army but the marines, too, and fooled everyone. Then when the war was over, she boldly petitioned the military authorities and demanded a pension of a shilling a day."

Robert laughed. Lucinda was glad to see him looking cheerful once more. "And is this what you are planning to do, Lucinda? Run away to join the Army?"

"I? Why Robert, do not be foolish. Why should you imagine that I am preparing to emulate Hannah Snell?"

He studied her, his head on one side. "You have been strangely quiet and out of sorts recently, Lucinda. Mama is convinced you are pining for Mr. Somerford, but I know better."

Lucinda sought to set his mind at rest. Goodness knew what Robert imagined she might be plotting. And it was important that not even her beloved brother should gain wind of the truth about Miles and herself. She simply could not risk Robert's good-natured, well-meaning interference.

"Oh, I am sad because Melanie has gone," she declared. "And I freely admit, I am conniving ways to divert Mr. Somerford from asking me to marry him. The trouble is, however rude and unpleasant I am to him, the more determined he becomes. Yet I dare not try the opposite tactic of being sweet and docile, as for sure he will have me to the altar before you can say *Duke*."

"Yes, indeed," smiled Robert. "So you are attempting to blot it all from your mind by reading novels. I must confess, I rather admire your Hannah Snell. It has crossed my mind many times that the only solution would be for me to run away and join the Army. But on the meager allowance my father gives me, I could never hope to buy myself a commission and equipment and the means of transportation across the Channel."

Lucinda's eyes widened. "Robert, you speak in jest? You are not seriously contemplating running away?"

"I am in deadly earnest, my dear sister. But I cannot for the life of me imagine how my dream can be achieved. I have no income. And without the ready cash, I am tied, hand and foot, to Waverley Hall and those tedious books on animal husbandry."

He looked so forlorn that Lucinda's heart went out to him. Robert was a fine, upstanding young man, full of courage and vigor. It seemed to her shameful that he should be confined here, spending his days in useless argument with his father, when there was a war to be fought, and young, strong men needed to fight it.

Yet Robert was right. He could not just leap onto a horse and gallop away over the horizon in a headstrong, reckless manner. He must have the means to pay for his journey, his commission, and his fighting equipment.

That night, Lucinda lay awake for a long while, mulling over Robert's predicament. Somehow, she must help him. There must be a way. She tossed and turned between the sheets, thinking over all the possibilities. And then, long after midnight, when the only sound was the screech of the barn owls flitting ghostlike through the trees, Lucinda found the answer.

Excited, she sat up in bed, hugging her knees. Of course! Now she knew how she could find Robert the cash he required. And the beauty of it was, that no one need ever know how or where she had secured the money!

It would not, of course, be easy. In fact, there would be considerable personal danger involved. But Lucinda was prepared to face any adversity if it would assist her brother. If her plan succeeded, it would mean losing Robert . . . her one last remaining ally against the horrors of marriage to Charles Somerford.

Unselfishly, Lucinda put that thought behind her. If Robert remained in this house much longer, he would be totally stifled. He had to escape. His dream of joining the Army and fighting with the Duke of Wellington against the French must be fulfilled. And she, Lucinda, knew now how all this could be achieved.

If only, she thought, if only I can summon the courage!

SEVEN

Lucinda fell asleep with her mind in a whirl. She knew that the testing time would come the instant she awoke.

All her life, those first few waking moments had decreed whether or not she had made the right decision about any problem that was worrying her. If she opened her eyes and felt calm, as if a great weight had been lifted from her mind, then she was sure her conclusions of the previous night had been right. But if she awoke feeling fretful and disturbed, it meant she must think again and find a new solution.

This particular April morning, Lucinda drifted into consciousness and realized she felt as if she were floating on a cloud. All her instincts told her that the plan she had formulated long into the night was the right answer to Robert's problem.

As if to enhance her sense of optimism, the rain had stopped. Joyfully, she flung back the damask curtains and held out her arms in welcome to the sunshine that flooded into her room.

After breakfast—at which Lord Waverley made favorable comment on her cheerful countenance—Lucinda slipped away and made her way up to the picture gallery. She walked swiftly past the somber portraits, the bronze statues and gold-framed miniatures, until she came to the portrait of Ellen Fitzjohn.

As she studied the girl's lovely face, the defiant toss of those golden curls, and the passionate expression in the violet eyes, Lucinda recalled what Mrs. Trotter had told her. . . .

How Ellen's attempt to elope with her penniless lover had been foiled by her father. Lord Fitzjohn had slain Ellen's lover, whereupon the distraught girl had seized the sword and thrown herself upon the point.

Grief-stricken, and overcome with guilt, Lord Fitzjohn had decreed in his will that the summer house must always be guarded. No one must ever enter it again. And local folk whisper that Ellen hid some gold there, which she was planning to take with her when she eloped.

Robert shall have that gold! Lucinda thought fervently. I am sure poor Ellen would not mind. After all, it is in a worthy cause, and she was an ancestor of mine. I am convinced she would understand.

Mrs. Trotter had said that on scented

spring nights, the ghost of Ellen Fitzjohn sometimes appeared at the summer house.

"But on this occasion, the ghost of Ellen
Fitzjohn will be none other than myself,"
breathed Lucinda. "Mrs. Trotter's son Tom
guards the summer house every night. I know it
is unkind to scare him into running away, but
Tom is a resilient lad . . . and what a story it
will make to tell his friends, and eventually his
grandchildren."

Lucinda could not avoid the chilling
thought that perhaps there really was a ghost
who haunted the summer house of Medlow
Grange. That while she was occupied frighten-
ing Tom away, and entering the summer house,
the real ghost of Ellen Fitzjohn would appear . . .

She gazed once more into the beautiful
eyes of the portrait. "Please understand," she
pleaded, "I must do this for my brother. If he
stays much longer in this house, his spirit will
be broken . . . his youth and vigor lost. I must
help him to reach France, and Wellington's
forces. Then, when he has tasted life to the full,
he will be ready to return to Waverley and settle down as my father wishes."

The brilliant amethyst eyes of Ellen Fitzjohn stared back at her. For a moment, there in
the gloom of the gallery, it seemed to Lucinda
that the eyes came to life, sending a glowing
message of sympathy and understanding.

"There you are, Lucinda," came Robert's
voice behind her. "I have been searching all
over the house for you."

Lucinda whirled around, thankful that Robert was too far away to detect her guilty expression.

"Mama wishes you to join her," Robert went on. "The dressmaker is downstairs, with some muslins for your new summer dresses."

"I shall go at once," promised Lucinda, bidding a swift, silent, farewell to Ellen. "What are you doing today, brother?"

He grimaced. "I am to be instructed in the art of hedging. The merits of beech over hawthorn." He sighed. "What a waste of time! There I shall be, docilely examining hedgerows, and meanwhile across the Channel there is a war being fought!"

Patience, Robert, thought Lucinda as she hastened to the morning room. This tedious life will soon be over for you, my dearest brother.

While she discussed with her mother the merits of the sprigged muslin over the plain white, and whether waistlines were higher this year than last, Lucinda remained absorbed in her own private plans.

Reluctantly, she had decided against taking Robert into her confidence. It was a difficult decision. On the one hand, Robert had a right to be privy to her plans, as they were all to be for his benefit. And as she would be compelled to steal the gold under cover of darkness, it would be advantageous to have his help, company, and protection.

On the other hand, Lucinda dared not risk implicating Robert in the plan, for fear that something might go wrong and they were discovered in the act of taking the gold. If she were on her own, she could excuse the episode as a girlish prank. After all, what need could she have of all that money?

But if Robert were with her, the consequences for him would be far more serious. It was an open secret that Robert was dissatisfied with his allowance. He and his father argued constantly about the matter . . . almost as much as they clashed over the notion of Robert's joining the Army. Lord Waverley was a shrewd man. It would not take him long to put two and two together and realize that Robert wanted the gold to take him away to France.

No, Lucinda decided, I am better off on my own. The only remaining problem to be solved was when she should make her journey to Medlow Grange. It was a mere five miles away, no great distance on horseback. The difficulty was —how could she travel unobserved, and at night?

It was not until the muslins had been cleared away and the dressmarker had departed that Lucinda was given her answer. Cook came into the morning room to discuss the week's menus with her mistress.

"If you please, my lady, I would be most grateful if we could arrange to have a cold dinner on the evening of April 30."

Lady Waverley looked puzzled. "April 30? Why . . . ?" Then her brow cleared. "But of course. It is known as May Eve, is it not?"

Cook nodded. "That's right, my lady. You know how it is with all the young people in the village. They take a picnic, and go off into the woods to cut down the May blossom. Look forward to it all year, they do."

"I must confess," said Lady Waverley, smiling indulgently, "I have never understood why they have to wait until it is dark before they gather the *May* boughs. Surely if they went in the daytime, they would be able to see the blooms more easily?"

Cook cleared her throat and focused her eyes vaguely into the middle distance.

Lucinda said hastily, "I believe, Mama, that they find it amusing to light a fire in the woods and dance around it. During the daylight hours, it would seem less of an adventure."

In reality, Lucinda knew, the lads and lassies of the village had more important things on their mind than the lighting of bonfires on May Eve. For it was, by tradition, the night when courtships began. A magical time when convention was cast to the wind and they could run free in the woods with the boy or girl of their choice, there to join hands and kiss beneath the scented clouds of May blossom.

Lady Waverley sighed, "Well, I suppose as Lord Waverley is such a stickler for tradition, he can hardly complain if we give the younger servants the evening off in order that they may pursue a custom that has been prevalent for centuries." She inclined her head at Cook. "Very well. I shall write out a menu for a cold repast that evening."

Lucinda drifted out into the garden, her eyes alight with triumph. Of course, May Eve would provide her with the perfect cover for the ride to Medlow Grange. It was the one night of the year when the woods and fields would be alive with laughing young people. It would be simplicity itself to lose herself in the throng. Providing she was not missed from the house, then no one would notice her mingling with the village lads and lasses.

Despite his assertion that of course the servants must be allowed to enjoy their traditional customs, Lord Waverley was extremely grumpy when presented with his May Eve dinner: pickled herrings in soured cream, cold beef pie, and fruit trifle.

"A body needs hot food to keep it fuelled," he maintained testily, examining a chunk of beef as if it had been poisoned.

"Simple fare will do you no harm for once," declared Lady Waverley stoutly.

The Earl pushed the rest of the pie to the side of his plate. "I can feel all that cold pastry settling in a nasty lump at the bottom of my stomach. I am convinced I shall have indigestion tonight."

"Have another glass of claret, sir," suggested Robert, passing the decanter. "It is a wonderful aid to the digestion." He turned to his sister. "Would you care for a game of backgammon after dinner, Lucinda?"

She raised a delicate hand to her head. "Thank you, Robert, but I feel rather out of sorts. Just a headache, but I think I will retire to bed straight after dinner."

"I will have one of my new powders sent up to you," said Lady Waverley anxiously.

"No, no," said Lucinda, attempting to look

wan. "I should much prefer just to rest in the dark. I have little faith in powders."

As she anticipated, this brought her father to her aid. "Quite right," he grunted. "I'm glad to see you're getting some sense into your pretty head at last, Lucinda. All these new medicaments are a waste of time."

Seeing that Robert was ready to prolong the argument, Lucinda rose quickly to her feet, made her excuses and good nights, and fled from the room. Distantly, from the kitchens, she could hear the sound of laughter as the younger servants prepared for their night of revels in the woods.

What I have to do now, she thought, is wait, as patiently as I can!

By the time the church clock struck nine, all was silent at Waverley Hall. Lucinda imagined her mother quietly sewing in the drawing room, while her father sipped his port in the library nearby. Robert, doubtless, had retired to his chamber, to read his latest copy of *The Gentleman's Magazine*.

The hours that followed her removal from the dining room had seemed endless to Lucinda. But she knew she could not possibly have sat downstairs playing backgammon with Robert without her eyes revealing something of her inner excitement. It would have been fatal for Robert to suspect her plans at this late stage.

Now the time had come! Softly, Lucinda slipped from her room and ran down the back stairs, leaving the Hall by the garden door. From there she made her way around to the stables, where her faithful mare stood quietly in her stall. Lucinda had decided that this was an occasion when she must ride bareback, for it would take too many precious minutes to saddle the horse. Besides, she could not risk waking the stableboys who slept in the loft above.

Speaking soothingly to the mare, Lucinda fastened on the bridle and led her out into the courtyard. As in the way with horses, the mare seemed fully to understand the need for secrecy. She trod lightly across the cobbles, her hooves making the barest sound. Once clear of the stables, Lucinda gathered up her skirts and flung herself onto the mare's back.

"Good girl," she breathed, stroking the soft, glossy coat and urging the horse forward toward the lane which led to Waverley village.

Lucinda was clad in a white muslin dress, over which she had thrown a simple cotton cloak. Admittedly, she knew that at close range she looked every inch the lady she really was, but hoped that under cover of the darkness her appearance would not differ too much from that of the village girls.

She rode down the lane and through the pretty village, following then the sounds of laughter coming from the wood that fringed the hillside. Ahead was a group of lads and lasses who had joined hands and were dancing along the road. Lucinda slipped down from her mare and joined them.

They were in high spirits. Some carried hampers of food, others blankets to spread while they ate their picnic around the fire in the woods. The younger children ran ahead in noisy packs, for it was traditional that even they were allowed to join the revels, falling asleep on the blankets while their elder brothers and sisters kissed in the shadows.

Lucinda envied them their lighthearted gaiety as they entered the woods and ran amongst the May trees, filling their baskets with blossom. Tomorrow they would take the laden branches home and decorate the entire village with the white flowers, ready for the May Day celebrations.

How Lucinda longed to run and gather May blossom with them! But she had a more important task ahead of her. Leading the mare, she followed the path through the trees, and then remounted, leaving the merrymaking behind her. Ahead were spread two broad fields and beyond them, just visible in the moonlight, lay the ruins of Medlow Grange.

The house had been gutted by fire long ago, leaving naught but a ghostly gray shell. It was as if, Lucinda reflected, after Ellen's death Medlow Grange had been fated. The walls surrounding the grounds were crumbling, and the lawns and gardens sadly overgrown. Lucinda turned the mare away from the house, and along a weed-tangled path that led to a small clump of trees.

The light of the moon barely penetrated through the canopy of leaves and branches. For the first time, Lucinda began to feel afraid. An owl screeched somewhere overhead. A bat brushed by her cheek in the darkness. The creatures of the night were summoning their forces against her, the intruder. Lucinda shivered, uneasily aware of resentful eyes watching her from the trees.

She jumped down from the horse and tethered her securely to a tree. She also tied her cotton cloak to a branch, leaving herself dressed in the muslin gown and lacy white shawl.

As a final contribution toward her ghost-like appearance, Lucinda lifted her hands and removed the pins from her hair, allowing her golden curls to cascade free and wild around her shoulders. Now she was ready!

Treading warily, she left the little wood and positioned herself behind a clump of rhododendron bushes. Their thick, finger-like leaves formed sinister patterns in the darkness, but Lucinda refused to listen to the fearful hammering of her heart. For ahead of her lay the summer house.

It was smothered with ivy which had been allowed to grow unchecked over the door and windows. Yet the long grass roundabout had been cut, and recently, too, judging by the sweet fragrance lingering in the night air. That was probably thanks to Tom Trotter, Lucinda decided, occupying himself with the scythe during the long, lonely nights in the grounds of Medlow Grange.

She could see Tom now, sitting with his back to the summer house, eating hunks of bread and cheese. Lucinda imagined his mother packing it up for him in a clean white cloth, along with a slice of her delicious cinnamon cake.

"Poor Tom," Lucinda whispered, "I really

am sorry to be upsetting you . . . and spoiling your supper, too."

But she knew that if she did not act now, her courage would fail her. Searching amongst the rhododendrons, she selected a couple of heavy stones. These she threw, with the accurate aim learned from Robert in childhood, to land on the roof of the summer house.

As the stones clattered onto the only part of the tiled roof not choked by ivy, Tom dropped his bread and cheese and leaped to his feet. Lucinda watched him walk suspiciously around the summer house, trying to find the cause of the disturbance. As soon as he reappeared, she threw back her lovely head and glided, soft and silent, down the hill toward him.

Tom, looking up, stood transfixed, the scream dying in his throat. With the moon shining full upon her, the swaths of white shawl and muslin dress floating in the breeze, Lucinda was an exquisite vision of white and silver and gold.

As Tom stared, the apparition raised her arms, like a fair-haired avenging angel come to seek justice. Tom waited no longer. He—who had always stoutly maintained that he did not believe in ghosts—turned and fled.

Thank heaven for that, thought the ghost, listening to his dying footsteps with considerable relief. She ran to the summer house, but drew back at once in dismay. There on the door was a large, solid lock.

"How stupid of me!" exclaimed Lucinda.

"Why did I not anticipate that the summer house would be locked? But I will not be beaten! There must be a way in somewhere."

Inch by inch, Lucinda felt her way around the sides of the summer house, plunging her hands through the stranglehold of ivy to the cold walls beneath. At last, she found what she was looking for. Tearing away the creeper, she revealed the rotting framework of a window. It was crusted with dirt, and within minutes Lucinda's hands, face, and clothes were filthy. But she cared not. Within minutes she had pried apart the rusty catch, and pushed the creaking window wide enough to enable her to scramble through.

She landed on a cold, tiled floor. The summer house smelt musty and airless. It was pitch dark, but Lucinda had come prepared for that. Neatly secured in the deep hem of her dress was a candle and a small tinderbox. She lit the candle, placing it carefully in an old earthenware flowerpot she found lying on the tiles. Then holding the light aloft, she began her inspection of the place which had witnessed such terrible deeds committed within its walls.

How well she could imagine the meeting between Ellen and her lover. Here was a wicker table, and there a cane seat just large enough for two. Lucinda visualized the seat piled with cushions and the lovely Ellen lying in her lover's embrace, her face kissed by the moonlight streaming through the window.

Lowering her candle, Lucinda noticed an irregular, dark brown stain on the floor. She froze. It must be the blood of the lovers, mingled together in a permanent reminder of their tragic death.

The thought drove Lucinda into action. I must not tarry, she told herself. If Tom runs back to Waverley and raises the alarm about the Medlow Grange ghost, it is possible that he may form a party to come and investigate. I must hurry!

The gold, Mrs. Trotter had said, had been hidden by Ellen beneath the floor of the summer house. Lucinda gazed helplessly at the tiles. Where should she start? It would take her all night to lift each of these tiles, for they were heavy and deeply embedded in the earth.

Lucinda refused to allow herself to panic. "Think, Lucinda," she instructed herself sternly. "If you were Ellen, where would you bury the gold?"

Calmly, Lucinda carried her candle from one side of the summer house to the other as she studied the tiles. It was then she noticed that all the tiles were fashioned from red clay . . . except one, almost hidden in the corner farthest from the door. This single tile was made of mellow sandstone.

Acting on a pure, sure instinct, Lucinda set the candle down and took a penknife from the hem of her gown. Carefully, she chiselled out the earth from the side of the yellow tile. By the time she had finished, her elegant nails were ruined, while her hands were roughened and bleeding.

Oblivious of the pain from her smarting fingers, Lucinda gathered up all her strength and began to pry the tile from the floor. At her first attempt she fell back, exhausted. But she carried on and eventually she felt it move. Encouraged, she took a firm grip and pulled with a vigor she never knew she possessed. At last, the tile was safely removed and she was looking down into a hollowed-out space.

With her breath coming in short, excited gasps, Lucinda saw the leather bag lying in the space beneath the floor. She lifted it out. It was monstrously heavy. It must be the gold!

Trembling with anticipation, Lucinda felt inside the bag and drew out a gleaming old piece. She had found it! Ellen's gold was hers, and soon Robert would be free to live the life he chose.

She held the piece of gold, cool and shining, against her burning cheek. And it was then that Lucinda became aware that she was not alone in the summer house.

Quite what alerted her, she never knew. Small sounds . . . the creak of the window, a soft step, a muffled movement. Terrified, Lucinda pushed the bag of gold back into the hollow and snuffed out her candle.

As she did so, there came the unmistakable sound of a tinderbox being scraped. Another candle flared into life revealing the silhouette of a man standing to one side of the window.

Lucinda's first instinct was to scream and run. But run where? Her only means of escape was the window, and the man was standing there, barring her way. She was trapped.

Trapped, but not defeated. She thought of

her brother and his need for the gold. Her courage came flooding back. No, she would not allow anyone to deter her now. She had no notion who this intruder might be, but *intruder* was an apt name for him. He had no right to be here. She, after all, was a descendant of Ellen Fitzjohn. But this man, standing still, silent, and sinister by the window, was clearly a rogue. Very well, she resolved. I shall frighten him away, as I frightened Tom!

Drawing up her shawl, she wound it around her face and glided slowly toward the man, praying he could not hear the distinctly unghostlike thumping of her heart. He stayed quite immobile until the apparition was within two feet of him. And then, to her consternation, he did the worst thing possible. He laughed.

Yet is was a laugh Lucinda recognized. An unmistakable, mocking sound that she had heard several times before. Confused, she dropped her shawl, and as her fingers relaxed, the gold coin clattered onto the tiled floor.

Miles bowed. "Good evening, my dear Lady Lucinda."

Recovering swiftly from her fear and surprise, Lucinda said with more than a touch of annoyance, "I might have known it would be you! How dare you laugh at me like that! You were supposed to be terrified in the face of Ellen Fitzjohn's ghost."

Miles smiled, and as he lifted his candle Lucinda observed that still he had not removed his mask. "I confess, Lucinda, I am not all that familiar with the ways of ghosts. Even so, I am positive that genuine apparitions do not wear dirt-streaked dresses or have cobwebs and ivy in their hair."

Lucinda sighed. "Oh, I had forgotten what a trouble it was breaking in here."

"And may I inquire," said Miles pleasantly, "just what you *are* doing here?"

For a moment, Lucinda contemplated not telling him the truth. But there was something so compelling about Miles that she knew she could not lie to him. Besides, he had heard the gold coin fall to the floor.

Stooping, she lifted the leather bag of gold. "I came for this," she said defiantly.

"Did you now?" replied Miles. "What a coincidence. For so did I."

She stared up at him, appalled, suddenly aware of his superior strength and power.

"But I need it," she blurted. "For my brother Robert. He is desperate to join our Army in Europe."

"How very strange," said Miles softly, "for that is exactly why I, too, require the gold."

Lucinda felt as if he had dealt her a physical blow. "You . . . you are going away?" she whispered.

He nodded. "In about six weeks' time. My affairs are almost settled in England, and I wish to fight for my country."

Lucinda sensed that she was being torn in two. How brave of Miles to wish to join the battle against the hated French. But how could she bear the thought that he was no longer in England, that he was in the midst of the bloody fray, perhaps wounded, on some alien, foreign field?

Gripping the bag of gold tightly, she backed away from him.

"You shall not have it!" she declared fiercely. "I found it first! I have a right to it. Ellen Fitzjohn was an ancestor of mine. She was nothing to you. And I need the money for my brother!"

"All indisputably true," said Miles calmly, his gray eyes glittering like steel in the light of the flickering candle. "But I am, for the moment, regrettably short of funds. The gold must be mine."

As he spoke, he advanced toward her. Quite suddenly, he pounced, seizing the leather bag. She snatched at his arm, kicking and clawing at him in a total frenzy.

"No! Give it to me, you beast, you rogue!"

He was strong and easily fended her off. As the tears streamed down her begrimed face, Lucinda unexpectedly found herself held in his arms.

"My dearest, bravest girl," he was saying tenderly. "Of course I will not take all the gold from you. There is enough here for both your brother and me. Here, we shall share it out."

He tipped the gleaming coins onto the floor and divided them until in one pile there were twenty-one, and in the other twenty. He scooped the twenty-one into the leather bag, and pressed it into her trembling hand.

"Take these for your brother," he said.

"But you have one less," murmured Lucinda, feeling calmer now.

"As I recollect, you dropped one," he said. "Ah, here it is, under the table." He handed it to her. "This coin is for you. As a memento of this episode, and our previous adventures together. I should hate you to forget me, Lucinda."

She felt too forlorn to speak. At last she whispered, "You mean, I shall never see you again?"

"Next month I am going away to war," he replied. "Anything could befall me. Keep the gold piece, Lucinda, and when you gaze upon it, remember me and the times we have shared."

She opened her mouth to protest, to plead with him not to go into battle and leave her. But already he was replacing the yellow tile, snuffing out the candle, and making ready for them to leave.

"Where did you tether your horse?" he asked.

"In the wood at the top of the hill," she replied miserably.

Gently, Miles lifted her through the window and then pulled the ivy back over the frame, leaving the summer house to mourn amongst its memories once more. He collected his own horse from a nearby secluded thicket, then accompanied Lucinda up the hill and assisted her onto her faithful mare.

"So you are riding bareback?" he said admiringly. "What a woman of rare accomplishment you are, Lucinda."

She could not find the words to reply. She was too sadly aware that this was the last ride she would ever take with her masked gallant,

Together, they crossed the fields and entered the woods where drifts of white May blossom scented the air and lovers kissed beneath the trees. Already, the strongest boys had cut down the tallest May tree, ready to take back to the village tomorrow to be garlanded with ribbons, in pride of place during the May Day celebrations.

The air was heady with romance, increasing Lucinda's sense of melancholy and loss. The man she loved was leaving her! Her great adventure was all but over. All she had to look forward to was a wretched marriage to a man she loathed.

When they reached the stable gate of Waverley Hall, Miles lifted her down from the mare. "This is where we must part," he murmured.

She gazed up at him, her eyes misty with tears.

"Farewell, Lucinda," he said softly. "Keep the gold piece I gave you, and think of me sometimes."

"I shall think of you always," she breathed.

His eyes held hers for a long, dreamlike moment. Then, swiftly, he bent and kissed her very lightly on the lips. For a second it seemed as if he was about to say more. But instead he turned abruptly and leaped onto his horse.

He raised his hand in a final salute and then disappeared into the night, leaving the desolate Lucinda with only her memories and the burning touch of his lips on hers.

EIGHT

"I just can't believe it!" exclaimed Robert. "Lucinda, I am lost for words . . . how can I ever thank you?"

Lucinda and Robert were closeted in their private refuge, the old nursery. Before them on the floor lay the twenty-one gold coins.

"To think," Robert went on, utterly bemused, "you went alone at night to that haunted summer house. Why, all manner of dreadful things could have befallen you!"

Lucinda pushed back her curls and murmured, with considerable understatement, "I confess, there were moments when my heart seemed to stop . . . but all was well in the end."

"I wish you had told me what you were planning," said Robert. "I would never have permitted you to go alone. In fact, I would have insisted on fetching the gold myself, leaving you tucked up safe and warm in bed."

Lucinda giggled. "But Robert, what a hulking ghost you would have made! Why, you are six feet tall and powerfully built. And even if you had worn a long curled wig, to be sure it would have blown off in the breeze!"

Robert grinned. "You are probably right. But when I think what you endured . . . the risks you ran, my dearest sister, just for me . . . I am . . . well, words fail me."

"Say nothing," said Lucinda, pressing his hand warmly. "I desire only that you should be happy. When do you think you will be able to leave?"

Robert's face lit up as he considered his plans. "I have friends at Dover who can arrange a fast passage for me. I shall send a messenger to them posthaste, and with luck I shall have all the arrangements completed within a week. Oh Lucinda, just imagine! This time next month I shall be wearing my hussar's uniform, galloping into action against the French!"

And you will not be alone, mused Lucinda, her thoughts straying sadly to a tall, dark man who would also shortly be fighting for his country.

Lucinda was sure her parents' suspicions must be aroused as, during the following week, an astounding change came over their younger son. Gone was the listless, melancholy expression. Instead he wore a permanent smile and strode about the Waverley estate with a purposeful air, his shoulders back and his eyes full of bright expectation.

At last, Robert's arrangements were completed. He planned to slip from the house as soon as his parents had retired and gallop through the night, changing horses along the way, reaching Dover at dawn. There was a packet leaving with the early tide, he told Lucinda, so by breakfast time, when his absence was discovered at Waverley, he would be on his way across the channel—and safe.

On the fateful night, he crept along to Lucinda's room to bid her farewell. This time, Lucinda found it impossible to check her tears.

"Oh, Robert," she sobbed, clinging to him, "I know it is best for you to go. But I shall miss you so!"

"And I, too, shall miss you, sister dear," he murmured. "I know I can never repay you for what you have done for me."

"Repay me by finding what you seek in life," she told him, her eyes bright with tears. "And by coming home safely."

He kissed her on both cheeks, then slipped swiftly from the room. Lucinda watched him from her window, the lone figure on a horse heading for Dover, and freedom and the unknown beyond.

The furor the next morning was even worse than Lucinda had imagined. At breakfast—the tone of which always laid the foundation for the remainder of Lord Waverley's day—Hill, the steward, handed him a note which Robert's valet had discovered in his chamber.

"Gone to join the Army!" exploded Lord Waverley. What confounded impertinence! The young scoundrel! I never *heard* of such a thing!"

Lucinda rushed to support her mother, who was swaying dangerously in her chair. "Hill, you must send a party to fetch him back, instantly," the Countess murmured.

Lord Waverley's fist smashed onto the table. "Too late. Too damned late! He's halfway across the Channel by now! It's outrageous! My word, if he ever dares show his face in this house again, I'll have him horsewhipped for his impudence. Disobeying my orders! Taking matters into his own hands ..."

"Come, Mama," Lucinda whispered. "Let me assist you into the garden. A breath of fresh air will revive you."

Lady Waverley agreed, being only too happy to escape from the dining room, for her lord was bellowing so loudly he was causing all the breakfast crockery to rattle.

What was urgently required, Lucinda realized, was a diversion—some fresh dramatic event to distract her father from Robert's *fait accompli*. Early that same afternoon, the diversion presented itself. But not in a form that was at all to Lucinda's liking.

Shortly after their light luncheon, Lady Waverley sought out her daughter in the music room, where she was practising on the pianoforte.

"Run and change your dress, Lucinda. Mr. Somerford has returned from London and come straight to wait on your father. Oh, Lucinda, it can only mean one thing!"

Reluctantly, Lucinda changed into her new muslin dress with the pretty embroidered hem and brushed her lovely hair until it shone. She was, she realized, about to face the most difficult half-hour of her life.

"So be it. But I may as well look presentable for my ordeal. And at least," she mused, with wry good humor, "what is to happen now will surely eclipse all Robert's misdemeanors."

On entering the drawing room, she found Charles Somerford already there, engaged in conversation with her mother. Lucinda dipped him a brief curtsey and kept her eyes steadily on the floor. She desired to look neither at Mr. Somerford, who repulsed her, nor at her mother, who, she knew, was attempting to send significant signals across the room.

"Lucinda," said Lady Waverley in a fussed voice, "Mr. Somerford has something to say to you. I . . . er . . . I have to speak to one of the housemaids now. The brasses on the front door, you know, have not been polished properly these last three days. I . . . will be in the morning room should you require me."

Charles Somerford wasted no time. No sooner were the drawing room doors closed behind Lady Waverley then he advanced towards Lucinda, declaring, "Lady Lucinda, your respected father has given me permission to address you. From the first, I have made my intentions clear on the matter of finding myself a wife. Not just any girl will do, you understand. For the future Duchess of Lexburgh I require a lady who will grace the title of Duchess and be a credit to me."

"Naturally," murmured Lucinda, wondering however she was going to manage to keep a straight face during this interview.

Charles Somerford paced back and forth between the fireplace and the windows.

"Lady Lucinda, the moment I set eyes on you, I was struck . . . nay, overcome . . . *overwhelmed* by your dazzling beauty. Yes, that's it, dazzling beauty. And . . . er . . . your exquiste deportment and . . . er . . . your air of . . . of delicate breeding."

Mr. Somerford was rapidly becoming red in the face and seemed to be having difficulty with his breathing. Fair words and fine compliments, Lucinda mused, clearly did not trip easily from his lips. From beneath her modestly lowered eyes, she watched him struggle for the right words. Was he, perhaps, about to compare her to an English rose?

"You are like a flower!" he said triumphantly. "A perfect summer rose, fresh with morning dew!"

But Mr. Somerford, she thought, biting back her laughter, I have no wish to bloom with you, in Derbyshire.

Encouraged by her maidenly silence, he continued, "Nothing would please . . . *honor* me more than if you would consent to become my wife."

Beads of perspiration were pebbling his brow. He regarded Lucinda anxiously, wondering if he had said enough. As Lucinda remained silent, he went on, "Of course, I realize that Derbyshire sounds a long way away. But your family will be more than welcome for the occasional visit. Come now, what do you say?"

Lucinda longed to tell him truthfully that this was the clumsiest and most unwished-for proposal she had ever had the misfortune to receive. But good manners dictated that she must give him a civil reply With considerable difficulty, she composed herself and gained control of her voice.

"Mr. Somerford," she said steadily, "I am most conscious of the honor you have bestowed upon me in desiring to make me your wife. But I fear that our union can never be."

Charles Somerford let out a long, exasperated sigh. "Lady Lucinda, I know you to be a spirited, intelligent girl. That is why I selected you. Now, bearing all this in mind, may we not dipsense with the formalities? I am aware that in polite circles it is considered proper for the young lady to demur, to reject the attentions of the suitor who in her secret heart she has every intention of accepting in the end. I came into this drawing room prepared, in all good faith, to make the flowery speech I felt the occasion demanded. But the time for games of this sort is now over. I should prefer you to speak to me plainly."

"Very well," said Lucinda, drawing a deep breath. "If that is what you wish, Mr. Somerford. But remember that it is only upon your own invitation and urging that I presume to address you in such a frank manner. I regard you as one of the least appealing men I have ever met. Your manners, your bearing, your appearance, and your character all repel me. I will not marry you, and furthermore, I wish you gone from my sight!"

His face was livid. His pale eyes bulged. In two strides he was beside her, gripping her arm. She tried to break free, but his fingers bit cruelly into her white skin.

"So," he breathed, "you dare to allege that I repulse you! Well, so be it. I am not marrying for love. That I freely admit. There are many other ladies in London who would do just as well as you. But I have already informed certain of my fashionable friends in the capital that you are to be my bride. I have no intention of returning with my tail between my legs to announce that you have refused me."

Lucinda tossed her head. "It seems you have no choice, Mr. Somerford."

"I would remind you that I have your father's consent for this marriage," hissed Charles Somerford. "I shall return and speak to you again, by which time I shall hope to find you in a more amenable frame of mind."

With that he bowed, turned on his heel, and rushed from the room.

A few moments later Lady Waverley bustled through the doors. "Lucinda, whatever happened between you? Why did Mr. Somerford leave so abruptly?"

"Because I rejected his offer of marriage," said Lucinda. She closed her eyes and waited for the parental storm to break.

Midafternoon saw Lucinda locked in her bedchamber. There she would stay, her furious father decreed, until she saw sense and agreed to marry Mr. Somerford. Lord Waverley had even gone so far as to declare that Lucinda was to have only bread and water for nourishment, but the entire household knew that this was mere bluster and that Lady Waverley herself would take up trays of food for her daughter.

It was such an ironical situation, reflected Lucinda as she arranged the cushions on her favorite windowseat. She had known that Mr. Somerford's proposal would provide the necessary diversion to divert her father's wrath from Robert. So far, so good. What she had not fully anticipated was the manner in which Robert's defection would serve to exacerbate Lord Waverley's fury toward her and make her own situation more wretched.

Lord Waverley had declaimed that his parental authority was being seriously undermined. First Robert took matters into his own hands and joined the Army (though God only knew, Lord Waverley muttered, how he had managed to finance his expedition) and now Lucinda was proving a rebellious, defiant little miss by refusing an excellent suitor. It wouldn't do. It wouldn't do *at all!*

Hence his drastic action in confining Lucinda to her room. Before a tearful Lady Waverley had locked the door, she had murmured, "Lucinda dear, I see no possibility of your father relenting. I fear you must make up your mind to marry Mr. Somerford . . . or all our lives will be made quite impossible."

Lucinda smiled now. Poor Mama. Papa would take a great deal of pacifying. The atmosphere downstairs would not be at all pleasant for some time to come.

But I simply cannot marry that dreadful man, thought Lucinda. I cannot commit my life, my future into his hands. It amazed her that her parents could not see what an undesirable person he was. Yet they are blinded, she mused, by his forthcoming title. My father desires to have a duchess for a daughter.

And after all, they have not seen Charles Somerford in the light that I have. In company, his manners are perfectly acceptable. But when he and I have been alone together, there has been something malicious and menacing in his eyes. A change has come over him, which is hard to explain in words, but which makes my flesh creep.

There was a coarseness about Charles Somerford that repulsed Lucinda—especially when she compared him to Miles. Miles was everything a man should be. Strong, rugged, forceful, yet in his dealings with her he had always been gentle. Right from the beginning, when he had swept her onto his horse and carried her off down the lane, he had been the perfect gentleman.

On the lakeland island she had been totally at his mercy. He had expressed a desire to kiss her . . . but he had not forced her. Lucinda had no doubt in her mind how Charles Somerford would have behaved in similar circumstances. Indeed, had he not given her evidence of his brutal, insensitive nature on that occasion near the river at Guildford?

Lucinda had found it quite impossible to phrase for her parents the exact reasons for her dislike of Charles Somerford, for much of her loathing was based purely on feminine intuition. She sensed an evil about him. But what?

In her parents' eyes, what wrong had he done her? He had attempted to compell her to kiss him, that was all. Hardly a serious crime, when all was said and done. From her parents' point of view, what was that single indiscretion when set against his position in society, his wealth, his total eligibility as a husband?

So what am I to do, murmured Lucinda, her head beginning to throb as she considered her position. Papa is adamant. He is determined that I shall marry Charles Somerford. But I know that I shall die in spirit if I am forced to become his bride.

It all seemed hopeless. Restlessly, Lucinda turned to plump up the windowseat cushions, conscious that something hard was jutting into her back. Feeling behind the velvet cusion, she remembered that she had hidden one of her novels there. Gazing on the title, her face brightened.

"Of course!" she gasped, hugging the book to her. Why, the solution to her dilemma lay here, right in her very hands! For the book she held was the tale of enterprising Hannah Snell's adventures as a female soldier.

Naturally, she could never attempt to emulate Hannah and really become a soldier. But what was to prevent her joining Miles when he went into the Army? The idea was not as preposterous as it might seem. After all, Lucinda reasoned, many women followed their men into war. It was an accepted practice. Not, admittedly, a *respectably* accepted practice, but Lucinda decided that a situation as desperate as this called for unorthodox methods to resolve it.

I love him, she thought fervently. He is the only man in the world with whom I desire to be. It is as if fate has driven us together. If Charles Somerford had not proposed, or my father been so adamant, I would never have dreamed of running away to be with Miles. Yet in the present circumstances, what other choice have I? To stay here at Waverley and marry a man I loathe? No, that can never be.

Miles has made me realize how intoxicating are the joys of freedom and adventure. And he would look after me, I know he would. I should take care not to be a burden to him. And how thrilling it would be!

Lucinda's imagination soared as she thought of travelling in foreign lands, hearing the beat of the drum and the blare of trumpets as the men rode into battle. She would become friendly with the other camp women, and they would spend their days preparing for the homecoming of their menfolk . . . and in the evenings there would be gatherings around the camp fires, and sing-songs, and endless glorious stories of their heroes' victories at war.

After all, mused Lucinda, her eyes luminous

with excitement, Robert has done it. And we are so alike. Why should not I be granted my freedom, too?

In the hours which followed, Lucinda could think of nothing to dissuade her from her plan. Or rather, she would allow no such discouraging thoughts to enter her mind. Miles had told her he could be found at the Blue Boar Inn on the Guildford road. She was in a frenzy of anticipation at the notion of seeing him again . . . and setting off with him on this wonderful adventure.

At seven o'clock, Lady Waverley unlocked the door and brought in a supper tray. "I cannot stay but a minute, Lucinda. Your father would make my life unbearable if he knew I was here. Have you had no change of heart yet, my dear?"

Lucinda shook her head. "I am sorry, Mama."

"You were always an obstinate girl when you took an idea into your head," sighed Lady Waverley. "But this time, Lucinda, you will not get your own way. Your father is determined to see you married to Mr. Somerford."

Lucinda was suddenly aware that this would be the last time she saw her mother for . . . how long? Perhaps forever. After all, when her father learned of what she had done, he would doubtless refuse to acknowledge her as his daughter. She would be barred from the house and from social intercourse with her family.

The thought sent a chill through her bones.

But then she imagined the alternative—marriage to Charles Somerford—and the fire of resolve kindled her courage once more.

"Dearest Mama," she said, taking her mother's hand, "you know I love you, don't you? And whatever I may do . . . remember it is for the best, and not to cause you grief."

Lady Waverley looked bewildered. "Being cooped up in this stuffy room is doing you no good, Lucinda. You are babbling. You will end up crazed. Now eat your supper. There is asparagus pie, your favorite fruit jelly, and some sweet biscuits. I had Cook make the jelly specially for you, though your father will dismiss her if ever he finds out."

Lucinda's eyes misted. "You are kind Mama. Try to think well of me."

"I shall see you in the morning," said her mother. "And do endeavor to see sense, Lucinda."

The key scraped once more in the lock, and Lucinda could hear the rustle of silk as her mother walked away. Lucinda was in too much of a tumult to feel hungry, but she forced herself to eat the pie and sweets on the tray. After all, she reasoned, I have no notion when my next meal may be. And I shall need all my strength in the hours after darkness.

She had plenty with which to occupy herself. First, there was the matter of joining the bedsheets and tying one end to the strong oak bedpost. Lucinda had learned from her novels that a sheet-rope was one of the simplest ways of escaping from an upstairs room in a house.

With that completed, Lucinda turned her

attention to the question of finance. She would undoubtedly need to take some money with her, both to pay for her everyday requirements and to buy her way out of any emergency that might arise.

But there lay the problem. She had no jewelry available, for Lord Waverley insisted that all the family valuables be kept locked in the library safe. And although Lucinda was a rich woman in her own right, all her wealth was invested in stocks and shares carefully administered by her brother Frederick.

Her father, naturally, paid all her bills. As she rarely went out into society, Lucinda had never before had need of any money. Yet now she found herself sorely embarrassed on this count.

How ridiculous, she mused, that the Lady Lucinda Verney has not a single shilling piece she can lay her hands on! Yet wait . . . I may not have a shilling . . . I have more than that. I have a *gold* piece!"

Hurrying to her dressing room, she rummaged in the bottom drawer of her tallboy. There, hidden beneath a discarded riding dress, lay the shining gold coin which Miles had given her on that fateful night at Medlow Grange.

Swiftly, she tucked it securely into the pocket inside the bosom of her dress. Its cool hardness against her skin felt as reassuring as a lucky talisman. While she was in possession of Miles's coin, she was sure no harm could befall her.

At last, she heard ten o'clock chime on the church clock. She forced herself to wait another quarter of an hour, until her parents would be safely in their apartments. Then, flinging on her cloak, she crossed to the window and gently eased it open.

She flung out the knotted bedsheets, noting with relief that she had judged correctly, and they almost reached the ground. Taking a deep breath, Lucinda prepared to make her escape.

The worst part of the exercise, she discovered, was the very first . . . actually clambering out backwards from the window and gathering the courage to let the linen sheets take her weight. Grimly, she clung on, not daring to look down. The hem of her dress ripped against the rough stone wall, whilst her knees and shins were badly scraped. But the sheets held, and gradually, moving hand over hand, she completed her descent.

At the bottom, she was trembling, but triumphant. The first stage was completed!

She wished she had been able to think of a way to remove the telltale sheet-rope, so her absence would not be discovered so early in the morning. All she could hope for was that Miles would spirit her away so swiftly that her father would have no hope of tracking them down.

There was no time to lose. Lucinda hurried around to the stables.

"Hello, there, my friend," she murmured to her mare. "You must be becoming accustomed to me coming at this time of night, to ride you bareback under the stars."

Once again, the faithful mare sensed her mood and her needs. Within minutes, they were crossing the stableyard. Then Lucinda was on the horse's back, heading toward the lane, following the same route taken by Robert when she had watched from her bedroom window and envied him his freedom.

But now, she thought exultantly, it is my turn!

As there was no moon, Lucinda decided against riding cross-country to Guildford. Instead, she boldly elected to take the road. It had the advantage of being the more direct route, but at the same time she was fully conscious of all the attendant dangers . . . the possibility of attack by highwaymen, brigands, rogues of all sorts who roamed the roads by night.

Yet because of the gold piece nestling against her bosom, Lucinda felt safe. Nothing, she was sure, could adversely happen to her whilest Miles's gold was hers. It would protect her as surely as he himself would guard her.

Miraculously, so it turned out, the only people she met on the road were two revellers, weaving along, soused with ale. One attempted to bow as she rode past, but the effects of the drink caused him to totter, and his good-natured companion only just prevented him from falling into the ditch.

Nevertheless, Lucinda felt a profound sense of relief when she saw the lights of the Blue Boar Inn twinkling ahead of her. Although it was nearly midnight, the Blue Boar was teeming with life. Sounds of music and laughter echoed from the rooms. Dogs yapped in the courtyard, and horses whinnied in their stalls.

Seeing her enter the courtyard of the inn, a groom ran out to take her horse. He gazed curiously at Lucinda. Despite her torn dress and bareback style of riding, she was clearly a lady. Yet arriving at this hour of the night. . . ?

"Shall I call the landlord, my lady? Do you require food, or a room?"

Lucinda said hastily, "Please do not trouble yourself. I am looking for a friend."

He nodded and said no more. It was then that Lucinda realized that the Blue Boar was not a totally respectable inn. The groom was trained not to ask questions. If ladies arrived on their own at midnight, looking for a "friend," then it was none of his business . . . unless someone paid him to divulge what he had witnessed. So he observed, and listened, but asked naught.

Seeing his shifty eyes upon her, Lucinda tried to give the appearance of knowing perfectly well where she was going. She pushed open one of the side doors and found herself in a gloomy corridor, lit by spluttering mutton fat candles.

Where, she wondered, would she find Miles? She had hoped to come across him quietly, to save herself the trouble and embarrassment of asking the landlord and alerting his suspicions.

At the end of the corridor a door was ajar, and she heard the sound of female laughter. Drawn by the noise, Lucinda paused in the shadows, gazing into a room where two women lounged on wooden settles.

From their appearance, Lucinda guessed that they were dancers. They were wearing colorful gypsy skirts, with tight-laced bodices in red and yellow. Their hair hung loose, tumbling over their bare shoulders, while their faces were vivid with rouge and paint.

One of the girls, with rather improbable red hair, was massaging her bare feet. "Oooh, I don't think I can dance another step tonight."

Her buxom friend downed her mug of ale and laughed, "I'll wager you won't have too much more dancing to do, Nell. From the way that masked man was looking at you earlier on, he'll have you off your feet and onto your back in no time."

Nell laughed coarsely. "Aye, he's a devil, that Miles. But what a man!"

Lucinda stood frozen in the doorway. How dared they talk of Miles, her Miles, in this common fashion?

"It'll be even more fun when we follow the fellows into the Army," said the raven-haired girl, holding up a glass and applying blacking to her lashes. "Just you and me, Nell, and all those dashing Army officers. What a time we'll have."

Nell grinned. "We won't be the only women, Tess. There'll be a camp full of us."

"But we'll be the only dancers," argued Tess, "so we'll attract most of the attention."

"Well, don't go throwing yourself at Miles," warned Nell. "He's mine."

Tess gave her a pert look. "For the moment, perhaps. But I know men of his sort. They are never content with just one woman. He's a man with a healthy appetite. He'll never be satisfied with just the likes of you."

Nell stood up, her eyes flashing angrily. It

was then that she noticed Lucinda, standing rooted to the spot in the doorway.

Lucinda turned to run, but Nell was too quick. Seizing her by the arm, she dragged her into the room.

"Well, well," she said grimly. "And just who may *you* be?"

NINE

While she had been listening to Nell and Tess, Lucinda had been forced into an agonizing reappraisal of her plight. How foolish—nay, how naive of her—to have imagined that Miles would welcome here with open arms and cheerfully carry her off to the war! She realized that she had completely misjudged not only the situation, but the very nature of the man she loved.

Lucinda understood now that their meetings, their adventures had indeed been merely make-believe . . . time out of time . . . enchanted hours when belief was suspended and magic ruled.

Here, now, at this tawdry inn, the stark reality lay before her. Miles was not a boy, like her brother Robert. Miles was a red-blood-ed man of the world. Though her cheeks burned, she compelled herself to accept that of course Miles must have known other women . . . many women, too, if Nell and Tess were to be believed.

With dreadful clarity, Lucinda now appreciated how she must have appeared to Miles —as nothing more than a bored girl in search of some harmless excitement. A wish which he had easily satisfied, before riding off again into the night, back to his real life and his real women.

But to Lucinda, those hours with Miles had meant everything. She had fallen hopelessly in love with him. Foolishly, she had persuaded herself that her love was returned. Now she saw that her expectations had been totally false. He had never intimated that he loved her. And of course he would never agree to take her off to the war with him. It was unthinkable. She would be a nuisance and an encumbrance to him. At least, the Lady Lucinda Verney would be an encumbrance. . . .

As Nell dragged her across the room, a fresh idea began to flower in Lucinda's mind. Coarsening her voice as best she could, she shook off Nell's hand and declared indignantly:

"Let me be, will you! I'm tired and thirsty, and I'd be glad of some of your ale."

Tess raised an eyebrow, but pushed across a tankard. Lucinda choked back her disgust at the smell and downed the sour liquid. Then she wiped a hand across her mouth. "That's better."

Nell threw herself down once more on the settle and inquired brusquely, "What's your name, then, and where are you come from at this time of night?"

"My name is Ellen," said Lucinda. "I come from a good family, but they cast me out after what you might call *a little trouble* with one of the Army officers stationed in our town."

Tess grinned. "Deary me. Naughty girl, were you?"

Lucinda shrugged. "You know how it is." From their knowing smiles it was evident that yes, they certainly did know. "I've been living by my wits, fending for myself. I can sing a bit, and I dance not too bad, as well."

"You're not dressed like a dancer," said Nell suspiciously.

Lucinda thought quickly. "No, I had to leave all my clothes in my last lodgings. A trifling matter of not being able to pay the landlord, you understand."

Nell shrieked with laughter. "So what are your plans now?"

"I'd like to team up with you, if you'll have me," said Lucinda boldly.

Tess walked slowly around Lucinda, her eyes critical, appraising. "Mmm," she said at last, "you're pretty as a picture, I must say. And your figure is good enough."

"I shall need a different dress," said Lucinda quickly. "I have money, if you'll let me buy some of your things."

"I thought you couldn't afford to pay the landlord?" Nell's voice was sharp.

Lucinda attempted a sly mile. "I wasn't going to give him my precious gold piece, was I?"

Nell darted to her feet. "You have gold? Show me!"

"Not so fast!" Lucinda backed away. "Say I may join you, and then you may see the gold."

Tess and Nell glanced at one another. Tess nodded. "Very well. There's a dress in that basket that will fit you."

As she spoke she held out her hand. Lucinda reached into her bodice and handed over the gold coin. A shiver ran through her. With the gold had gone her protection. Now she was totally on her own.

Tess hastily slipped the gold piece into her dress. "You'd better hurry and change. We're dancing for the gentlemen in the tavern in a few minutes. It will be your chance to prove yourself."

Lucinda threw off her muslin dress and put on a flame-colored gown with cross-laced bodice, tightly girdled waist, and skirts which swirled to her ankles.

"Mmm," said Nell. "Your face is too pale. Here, I'll rouge you."

Lucinda had never in her life put anything other than rosewater on her skin. How her mother would swoon with horror if she could see her now! Nevertheless, she stood still and submitted to Nell's artistic ministrations.

"There," said Nell, holding up a mirror, "isn't that better?"

Lucinda nearly recoiled as she regarded her alarmingly rosy cheeks and scarlet mouth. "Very pretty," she murmured.

Encouraged, Nell daubed a little more rouge in the cleavage of Lucinda's bosom. "Just as a finishing touch," laughed the red-haired girl.

There was a loud banging on the door, and the landlord called, "Are you ready, girls? The men are growing restive."

"Coming, don't fret yourself," shouted Tess. She winked at Lucinda. "They appreciate you all the more for waiting."

At the door, Nell paused. "Just one word of warning, Ellen. The handsome masked man sitting under the coaching clock is mine. Understand?"

Lucinda nodded. Her knees were trembling under the vividly colored skirts, and her bodice was laced so tight she could hardly breathe.

Tess led the way down the corridor, where a boy was standing outside one of the doors. She gave him a nod, and he darted inside, to alert the three fiddlers. Immediately, they struck up a merry, saucy tune, and then Lucinda felt Nell's hand in the small of her back, pushing her into the tavern.

At first, everything came as a blessed blur to Lucinda. She was dimly conscious of the men, sitting at rough wooden tables. Many had their feet up, some were banging their tankards in time to the music, while others were sitting back grinning expectantly at the three girls.

A space had been cleared in the middle of the floor for the dancing, but Lucinda had no idea what was required of her. Her knowledge of the dance was limited to the Roger de Coverley, the minuet, and of course the very daring waltz.

But the movements Tess and Nell were now

performing were far more outrageous than anything Lucinda had ever seen. How shamelessly they used their bodies, pushing forward their hips and bosoms as they whirled around the floor, moving so fast that their skirts lifted right up to their knees.

Lucinda saw Tess beckon, urging her to join the dancing. Crushing down her embarrassment, Lucinda stepped onto the floor. She had wanted excitement and adventure, and here it was. This was her new life. She could not be squeamish now. There was no going back.

Lifting her arms, Lucinda tossed back her head and flung herself into the frenzy of the dance.

How delighted the men were to see a new face! As Lucinda twirled past the tables, their hands reached out toward her. Feeling repulsed, and unclean, Lucinda danced even faster to avoid them. Seeing this, the men cheered and goaded her even more.

Lucinda dared not glance toward the men sitting beneath the coaching clock. She tried to confine her dancing to the other side of the tavern. But as the music and the mens' groping hands became more insistent, she found herself driven toward the one area she would have preferred to ignore.

Deliberately, she turned her back on the man in the corner. But as she turned past a neighboring table, a drunken lout arose and seized hold of her bodice. Lucinda tried to wrench herself away, but his grip was firm, his hand rough and relentless as it explored the soft contours of her swelling bosom.

What happened next occurred so fast that Lucinda hardly had time to draw breath. One moment she was struggling, helplessly, in the man's drunken, lascivious embrace. The next, he was sprawling back across the table and there were different hands seizing her shoulders.

Petrified, Lucinda gazed up into Miles's face. His eyes were cold, his mouth set in a hard, ruthless line. For a terrible moment, she thought he was about to strike her.

Instead, with what was clearly a monumental effort, he controlled his anger and pulled her instead through a side door. Roughly, he dragged her out onto the long grass at the back of the tavern, toward a gently trickling stream.

Lucinda stumbled alongside him, trying vainly to explain, "Miles—do not be angry—please understand—"

He would not answer. When they reached the stream, he forced her to her knees. Still he did not utter a word. Pulling out his handkerchief, he wetted it in the water, dragged back her head by the hair, and began to scrub the rouge from her face.

Lucinda cried out in protest, for he was hurting her. He only gripped her curls the harder and scoured her skin more viciously. When he had done, he threw down the handkerchief as if it were poisoned.

Lucinda was almost in tears. That he should treat her so! He, who had always approached her with such respect and gentle kindness!

Once more she attempted to speak, to explain. "Miles, I—"

He was staring down at her. From the light filtering out from the windows of the Blue Boar she noticed that his expression was strange, almost wild. As he regarded her tight-laced dress and heaving bosom a fresh torrent of rage seemed to consume him. Before Lucinda realized what was happening, he had seized hold of the neck of her bodice and in one stroke ripped it right away.

Lucinda screamed and tried to run. But he was too powerful for her. She writhed in his grasp while he, like a man possessed, furiously tore the thin material of her dress into strips, until it lay in flame-colored tatters on the ground. Lucinda stood before him, shivering in her flimsy chemise.

Suddenly, as he gazed upon her, a long, low cry broke from him. In a single, violent movement, he drew her to him and crushed her lips to his. It was a kiss that was almost savage in its intensity.

Her first kiss with Miles had been one of great tenderness. But never in her life had Lucinda experienced such a flood of emotions as were engulfing her now. The uncompromising masculinity of this man aroused in her a torrent of excitement that swept her headlong into ecstasy and inflamed her with a wild, consuming desire.

It ended as quickly as it had begun. Abruptly, Miles put her from him. For a moment, he stood with his hand covering his face, while he struggled to regain his composure. When at last he spoke, it was as if he was holding himself on a very tight leash. "Lucinda, my dearest Lucinda. How can you ever forgive me?"

"Miles, there is nothing to forgive," she said softly. And it was true. For her thudding heart, her heightened senses, her quickened blood told her that she had wanted Miles to kiss her in such a way. Not as a gentleman kissing a lady, but as a red-blooded man kissing a woman he desired. Yes, she had wanted it!

She went on, hesitantly, "You would not permit me to explain, Miles." Quickly, breathlessly, Lucinda outlined the circumstances which had led her to appear in such strange garb in the tavern of the Blue Boar.

When she had finished, Miles whispered, "My God. You will never know how shocked, how outraged I felt when I saw you like that . . . in that dress . . . with rouge on your face . . ."

Lucinda could not help remarking, "But Miles, my intelligence has it that you have favored the dancing girls in the past."

His face darkened. "You little fool, Lucinda! Can't you understand? Of course I have known many women. Ladies of fashion and others, too, women who were . . . well, less respectable. But for you, Lucinda, for *you* to appear before me dressed like a girl of the streets . . . why I felt as if I had been put upon the rack."

"I . . . I do not understand why *I* should affect you so," stammered Lucinda.

"Because I love you!" he declared, his voice shaking with passion. "Because you are the woman I prize above all others. You are beautiful. You have spirit. You are intelligent and brave and good. You are everything I have ever wanted in a woman. So you see, when I saw you in the garb of a common dancing girl, I felt half-crazed!"

Lucinda swayed, almost dizzy with joy. He loved her! Miles really loved her! Now all her problems were solved. Her eyes misted as she imagined her marriage to Miles, her happiness made even more complete by the knowledge that she would never have to set eyes on Charles Somerford again!

"Good heavens, Lucinda, how thoughtless of me," Miles's voice cut through her reverie. "Here you are standing in nothing but your chemise! You'll catch your death. Where did you leave your proper dress?"

"In the tavern. But the other girls will be there, and Nell will be furious with me. She had rather hoped to capture your attentions for herself this evening."

Miles grimaced. "Come, I shall escort you to the room." As he spoke, he slipped off his coat and wrapped it around Lucinda's slender shoulders. "Have no fear, Nell and Tess will not be there. I imagine they will be otherwise engaged elsewhere in the tavern by now."

Sure enough, the room was empty. Miles waited outside until she emerged, clad in her muslin dress and cloak.

"Come," he said, "we must make haste. Your mare is here, ready for you."

"Where are we going?" she enquired confidently.

"I am taking you home."

Lucinda stared up at him, stricken. "But, Miles, you do not understand. If I return to Waverley Hall, my father will force me to marry Charles Somerford. And I cannot. I cannot! I love you!"

Tenderly, Miles drew her to him. "And you are dearly loved in return, my precious Lucinda. Do you not think that I would sweep you off now and marry you at dawn if I could?"

"Then—" faltered Lucinda.

"I am not in a position to do so," he said, his voice grim. "Until my affairs are sorted out —which, pray God, will not take too much longer—I have no title, no house, and very little income to offer you."

"Let me come with you to join the Army!" pleaded Lucinda. "I promise I will be no trouble. I will learn to cook and care for you. I don't give a button for titles, or houses, or social position! All I want is you and to be with you!"

Later, Lucinda was amazed that she had made such a brazen speech. But there in that lonely courtyard, she felt consumed by the fever of love. She knew only that she could not bear to be parted from the only man she could ever love.

Miles held her tightly to him. "My dear, brave Lucinda. This is what I adore about you —this sense of adventure, this courage! But I am a man of honor. I have no wish to win you in an underhand fashion . . . and still less desire to cause alarm to your poor parents by whisking you away with me across the Channel."

Lucinda clung to him. "But, Miles, they will make me marry Mr. Somerford!"

Had Lucinda's face not been buried in Miles's broad chest, she would have seen his face darken, his eyes glitter ruthlessly. "I promise you," he said, his voice like chipped steel, "that you shall not marry Charles Somerford. You have my solemn word for it."

"But—"

He laid a hand over her lips. "Have I ever failed you?"

"No. Never."

"Then retain your trust in me. Now I am going to take you back to Waverley Hall. And this is what you must do. . . ."

An hour later, the masked man and Lucinda were standing outside Waverley Hall, where she was preparing to climb back into her room.

Miles shook his head in admiration as he viewed the knotted sheets hanging from her window. "You really are a girl after my own heart, Lucinda. Practically any other woman of my acquaintance would fall into a dead faint at the prospect of climbing up there."

She smiled wanly, dreading the thought not of the ascent, but of his departure. "Miles," she cried softly, "is there no way we may meet again before you leave for the war?"

"With all my heart I ache to see you before I leave," he murmured. "I shall be in London for the next few weeks. Perhaps I shall find a way."

Lucinda's heart sank. "London. Oh Miles, then we are doomed. I am never permitted to go to London."

"Do not despair." He smiled. "You should know by now that as far as we two are concerned, life and fate have a habit of playing strange tricks." He paused, and then continued in a low whisper, "But for the present, it is farewell. I long to kiss you again. But I confess, I dare not. My feelings for you are so strong, I fear for the consequences should I feel your sweet lips on mine once more."

For a long moment they gazed into one another's eyes. Then Miles lifted her high into the air, and Lucinda seized hold of the knotted sheets, to begin her ascent. He had advised her how to use her feet to take the strain from her hands. With Miles murmuring encouragement, Lucinda found the climb not too hard. When she had scrambled in through the window, and hauled up the sheets, she looked below and blew a kiss to the masked man.

Miles bowed. Then the man she loved turned and melted into the shadows.

Not surprisingly, Lucinda had a restless night and slept late the following morning. At half-past ten, she opened her eyes and, drawing back the bedcurtains, saw her mother approaching with a breakfast tray. Lucinda hastily pulled up the covers, so her mother would not observe the heavily creased sheets.

Lady Waverley smiled. "Your father is out with his bailiff this morning, so there is no need for me to lock the door. How are you today, Lucinda?"

"Hungry," declared her daughter, reflecting that this was hardly surprising, considering her exertions and excitement of the night before.

"And . . . er . . . have you had time to reflect, my dear, on this matter of your marriage?"

Lucinda laid down a forkful of cold beef and said demurely, "Yes, I have thought long and hard, Mama. I wonder, when Papa returns, do you think he would permit me a quarter-hour's conversation with him on the subject?"

Lady Waverley brightened. "Oh, to be sure! Does this mean you have relented? Will you be a good, dutiful girl and marry the man your father has chosen for you?"

Lucinda said, her eyes cast down so her mother would not see the laughter in them, "I realize that it is only right for me to be guided by my parents in this matter. There is, however, just one factor concerning the marriage that I should like to clarify with Papa."

"I cannot tell you how relieved I am," sighed Lady Waverley. "I had terrible nightmares, you know, imagining I should have to spend the next month creeping upstairs with trays of food for you. It would have been *so* inconvenient."

At midday, Lucinda curtseyed to her father in the library.

"So," he said, his voice gruff but not unkind, "you have come to your senses at last?"

Lucinda said carefully, following the speech she had rehearsed with Miles the night before, "I have no wish to go against your desires, Papa. If you wish me to marry Mr. Somerford, then I shall of course comply, in the most cheerful spirit."

Lord Waverley poured them each a glass of wine. "I am heartily glad to hear it, Lucinda. I had no desire to be harsh with you, you know. It wounded me deeply being compelled to act the ogre father. I want you only to be happy and well settled in life."

"I understand that, Papa," murmured Lucinda, "and I am deeply grateful for your concern."

"Then the matter is agreed," declared Lord Waverley. "It is all most satisfactory, as Mr. Somerford is to wait on us tomorrow morning. I understand that he is anxious to wed you speedily and take you back with him to Derbyshire."

"Of course, Papa." Lucinda leafed idly through one of the leather-bound books lying on the mahogany library table.

Lord Waverley went on, "It will be good for the Countess, having a wedding to arrange. It is a big day in a mother's life, you know, seeing her only daughter wed."

"To tell the truth," said Lucinda a trifle wistfully, "it is Mama I feel sorry for at this time."

Lord Waverley's bushy eyebrows rose in surprise. "Sorry, child? Why, pray?"

Lucinda smiled conspiratorially. "Of course, my marriage will be a great event for her. Yet I cannot help thinking how much more glorious it would be—from Mama's point of view—if I were marrying the Duke of Lexburgh, instead of plain Mr. Somerford."

Lord Waverley threw back his wine. "Well, Mr. Somerford *will* become a duke as soon as the lawyers have stopped fiddling around and the search is finally over for the old Duke's missing brother."

"As you say," sighed Lucinda, "the legal wrangling is nearly at an end. What a pity, then, that Mr. Somerford is in such haste for us to wed. If only he were prepared to delay for a few short months, then Mama would be granted the pleasure of seeing me become a duchess as the ring is slipped onto my finger. However," she said briskly, "it is not to be, so there is no point in wishing."

Lord Waverley paced up and down the book-lined room. Lucinda knew that, thanks to Miles, she had struck just the right chord.

"Lord Waverley is renowned as a lover of tradition," Miles had commented last night, when they had discussed the whole matter of her marriage of Charles Somerford. "And he has never made any secret of the fact that he wished his children to marry well. Your brother Frederick pleased your father by marrying the Lady Melanie. And one of the attractions of Charles Somerford's suit is that he hopes to inherit the title of Duke of Lexburgh. But from your father's point of view, with how much more prestige would the family be endowed if you married him when he became Duke, and was not merely the hopeful heir to the title."

So the plan had been formed. Miles had suggested the oblique approach through the pride of Lady Waverley, rather than a direct attack on her husband's well-known snobbery.

"Mmm," grunted Lord Waverley at last. "I confess I had not considered the matter from your dearest mother's point of view. But what you say makes sense. I shall explain to Mr. Somerford tomorrow that Lady Waverley would prefer to see her daughter marry a duke, and not a plain mister."

Lucinda nodded. "Whatever you think best, Papa. Now, if you will excuse me, it is my day for visiting the sick in the village."

Her father smiled. "You are a good girl, Lucinda. On your way out, be so good as to ask your mother to come and talk to me."

Lucinda sped quickly from the room lest he should observe the relief on her face. For the first time, she found herself positively looking forward to Charles Somerford's visit tomorrow!

At the appointed hour, Charles Somerford strode confidently into the drawing room where Lord and Lady Waverley and Lucinda were waiting to receive him. As was right and proper, Lucinda left the conversation to her father.

Mr. Somerford's changes of expression were wonderful for Lucinda to behold. When Lord Waverley announced that Lucinda had, on reflection, realized the honor Mr. Somerford was paying her, and would be delighted to accept his offer of marriage, Charles Somerford gleamed with triumph as he made the courteous responses that *indeed,* he was the one who was being honored, etc, etc.

However, as Lord Waverley proceeded to discuss the matter of Mr. Somerford's title, and the postponement of the nuptials, the pale blue eyes hardened. Lucinda watched him clenching and unclenching his fists. His voice grew tight and clipped. Yet before her parents, he dared not explode into the fury that clearly possessed him.

When their eyes met, Lucinda felt a chill of foreboding. Once again, she had outwitted him. But for how long?

He said, with forced grace, "Of course, Lord Waverley, I understand your feeling for your only daughter. Naturally, we shall wait until the legal affairs are settled and the title is mine. I am confident that it will not take long. And after that, there will be all the time in the world for the Lady Lucinda and I *fully* to enjoy one another's company."

Only Lucinda was aware of the implied menace in his words. What, she thought frantically, if all her plans went awry and she was indeed compelled to marry Charles Somerford? What would he do to her? Fearful scenes flashed through her mind, with Charles Somerford's sadistic temperament allowed full play. She would be his wife. He could do with her what he will. There would be no one to condemn him, and no one to protect her, for in law she would be his, to use or abuse as he saw fit.

All this was there, plainly writ for her to see in his cold blue eyes. Lucinda shivered and turned away from him.

At least, through Miles, she had gained some respite from this dreaded marriage. Oh, Miles, thought Lucinda fervently, I am now totally in your loving hands. Do not fail me now!

TEN

For the remaining weeks of May, the atmosphere at Waverley Hall was peaceful and harmonious. Lucinda, heady with relief that Charles Somerford had departed back to London, was in cheerful good spirits.

Her parents, too, were in a happy frame of mind. They rejoiced in their daughter's reformed attitude toward her marriage, and at the same time, Lord Waverley's initial fury over Robert's defection had now mellowed into an air of quiet pride.

Lady Falconbridge, in her forthright manner, had made the opinion of the entire county known on the subject:

"Dashed fine lad, your Robert," she declared, when she joined the Verney family for afternoon tea. "Everyone's talking about him, you know. Showed a high degree of courage and spirit, going off to fight for his country like that. Most impressive. I always said there was a lot more to Robert than anyone gave him credit for."

Lord Waverley huffed and puffed, but it was plain that, now he had had time to consider, he was indeed rather proud of his younger son. However, it was against his nature freely to admit this. Instead he commented gruffly, "Just hope the boy knows what he's doing. I don't mean just the filthy business of war. There's a great deal that goes with it, you know. All those camp women, for example. He could stray into bad paths."

Lucinda busied herself with her tea. How well she could imagine Tess or Nell enslaving the inexperienced Robert with their flattery and brash charm.

"Twaddle!" snorted Lady Falconbridge. "It will do Robert good to sow a few wild oats. He's of an age for it. And at least he'll have the decency to scatter them on foreign soil, and not sully our good English land!"

A flushed Lady Waverley coughed and rattled her teacup, casting warning glances toward Lucinda, who was staring fixedly out of the window.

"Now don't be so stuffy, Countess," declared the florid-faced visitor. "If Lucinda is to be wed, it is time she was made aware of the facts of life." She turned to Lucinda. "So you are set on marrying Charles Somerford, are you?"

"It has been settled, Lady Falconbridge," said Lucinda demurely.

"Mmm . . . I suppose you know what you're about. Can't say I took to the man myself."

"But Lady Falconbridge, you invited him to stay in your own house!" protested Lucinda's mother.

"Only because I am related, distantly, to his late wife, and felt it my duty to entertain Mr. Somerford," said Lady Falconbridge. "But I must speak my mind. It is my opinion that there is something definitely not quite right about Charles Somerford. Can't quite put my finger on it, but I never feel easy in his presence."

"Lady Falconbridge, you are referring to my future son," boomed Lord Waverley. "I would be obliged if you would either restrict your comments to those of a kindly nature or else keep them to yourself."

Lady Falconbridge shrugged, in a manner which Lady Waverley later decried as most unladylike, and the conversation turned to less controversial topics. Nevertheless, Lucinda was intrigued by Lady Falconbridge's forthright remarks. So she was not alone, then, in distrusting Charles Somerford!

"Such news, such news!" cried Lady Waverley, rushing into the dining room the following evening with a letter which had just come by special messenger.

"It is from Frederick. He writes to say that our dearest Melanie is with child!"

Lady Waverley was trembling so much she

could not keep on her reading glasses. The Earl was compelled to read the rest of the letter aloud to her.

"Frederick says that the child will be born in November."

Lady Waverley's hands flew to her face. "Oh! I must arrange for the nursery to be completely refurbished. And apartments must be made ready for Melanie's lying in. There will be so much to do!"

Lord Waverley read on, "The doctors have pronounced Melanie to be in good health, but Frederick comments that he has found her somewhat listless of late. Unfortunately, it is impossible for her to leave London until the end of the season next month. Frederick says she speaks often of Lucinda. He would be most grateful, in fact, if we could spare Lucinda for a few weeks, to visit Melanie in London and help to make some of the time of her confinement more tolerable."

Lucinda held her breath. She had no doubt at all that Miles was responsible for this turn of events! Of course, not even he had been able to foresee that Melanie would fortuitously be with child . . . but she guessed that the moment he had heard the news, he had seized upon it as an excuse to bring her to London, and to him! And Melanie, dear, sweet Melanie, had played her part to perfection, convincing Frederick that she needed Lucinda by her side.

But would her father agree? He hated London, though he had no objection to Frederick residing there, attending Parliament, and dealing with all the complicated matters relating to the Verney stocks and shares. But Frederick was an exception. Lord Waverley was most reluctant to allow any other member of his family to set foot in the capital.

Indeed, he at once began to demur. "I do not like the sound of this scheme for Lucinda to journey to London. I hardly think—"

"My lord!" Lady Waverley looked shocked. "How could you think of refusing poor Melanie such a request, and at such a time, too! Oh, how well I remember the tedium of my own confinements! Of course dearest Melanie longs for a companion of her own age and sex, and from her own family, too. It is only natural. I must insist that Lucinda be allowed to go!"

Lord Waverley's blue eyes widened in disbelief. Never, in their entire married life, had Lady Waverley insisted on anything. Stunned, he could do no more than murmur, "Of course, my dear. If you think it is best. Lucinda shall surely travel to London."

Lucinda could hardly believe that it had all been settled so easily. Lady Waverley, almost numb with shock at this unprecedented victory over her husband, swept Lucinda from the room. "Come, my dear. We must write express to Melanie."

There was so much to be done! The two ladies spent a week in a froth of arrangements, preparing Lucinda's clothes. Lucinda was adamant that the waistline on all her dresses must be lengthened.

"Did you not observe, Mama, when Melanie was here, her dresses were a whole inch lower in the waist than mine. It is clearly the fashion in London. I shall be laughed at as a rustic if I wear those gowns as they are."

Lucinda was glad she had so many preparations to occupy her, for the hours could not pass quickly enough before she set out for London. Nevertheless, excited as she was, she was careful to curb her anticipation in front of her father.

Loathing London so much, it was inconceivable to Lord Waverley that anyone should actually look forward to going there, and Lucinda had no desire to arouse his impatience by revealing her own jubilation. Prudently, she adopted the air of one who was travelling to London merely as a dutiful sister, to be by Melanie's side.

At last, the bright June day dawned. The carriage was waiting at the door, with her luggage loaded safely on top. After bidding a fond farewell to her parents, Lucinda set forth to the capital, escorted on the journey by Lord Waverly's stalwart steward, Hill.

It was the best of days for travelling. Under a clear blue sky the green hills and fields were starred with buttercups and daisies. Lucinda smiled as she relaxed against the cushions, happy in the knowledge that each turn of the carriage wheels was taking her nearer to Miles.

Toward three o'clock, Lucinda sat forward, gasping with delight as the magnificent London skyline came into view. How lovely it is, she thought, surveying the white silhouette of the ancient Tower, the soaring dome and glittering cross of St. Paul's, and the spires of all the

City churches. In the warmth of the afternoon sun, the mellow red brick of the City buildings glowed as if in warm, special welcome to Lucinda.

And within another hour, there was Melanie herself, standing at the door of her house on fashionable Curzon Street, holding out her hands in smiling greeting to her sister.

The two girls hugged and kissed. "Melanie, it is so good to see you. We are all overjoyed at your condition! Mama is beside herself with excitement, of course, and all the village women are busy sewing baby clothes." When Melanie had taken Lucinda into her drawing room and rung the bell for refreshments, Lucinda commented, "But how well you look, Melanie! Not at all pale and listless as we were led to believe from Frederick's letter."

Melanie laughed. "Your brother is out on Parliamentary business this afternoon, but he will be joining us for dinner. And of course I am in excellent health. I am sure you know why I arranged for you to come and stay?"

Lucinda said breathlessly, "Miles . . . has he been in touch with you? Do you know—"

Melanie raised a warning hand as a servant entered with tea and sugared cakes. "We shall talk tomorrow, Lucinda, I promise. Meanwhile, I am longing to know your opinion of the house. Frederick allowed me free rein in redecorating it. Although I had to be careful not to offend his traditional views, I think it is much improved, do you not?"

It was the first time Lucinda had visited Curzon Street since Frederick's marriage. She remembered it as a somber bachelor residence. But as Melanie led her on a tour of inspection, it was obvious that the gloomy atmosphere of old had been swept away. The walls were now lined with cream silk, while all the furnishings were light, graceful, and in exquisite taste. Melanie glowed with pride when Lucinda sincerely congratulated her on the transformation.

Frederick arrived home in good time for dinner at six. He was clearly pleased to see his sister, and agog to hear firsthand the details of what had come to be known in the family as "Robert's Army escapade."

Lucinda told him all she could, though it was evident from the gleam in Melanie's dark brown eyes that she suspected her sister of not revealing the entire story. How amazed she will be, thought Lucinda, when I tell her of my adventures at Medlow Grange!

"Papa is now really rather proud of Robert," Lucinda informed Frederick, "and Mama was reassured to receive a letter. He is fit and well, fighting with the hussars in the Rhinelands."

"Ah, the hussars. Everyone wishes to join the hussars," sighed Frederick. "Do you know, even the ladies of the *ton* have taken to wearing dark cloth pelisses, braided like the coat of a staff officer in the hussars."

"You will see these silly ladies tomorrow," Melanie told Lucinda, "sweltering in the June heat under the weight of all that dark cloth in their fashionable pelisses! I thought it would be pleasant, you see, if you and I went on a tour of the city."

Lucinda was happy to agree, and the chaise was ordered for nine o'clock. The two girls travelled first to St. James's, and Lucinda was delighted to renew her acquaintance with the red brick palace where she had been presented. From there, they journeyed down to Chelsea, where Lucinda admired the riverside homes set amidst the market gardens and a profusion of apple, plum, pear, and cherry trees.

The ride back beside the sparkling Thames was enchanting, although as they reentered the center of the city, Lucinda was alarmed by the traffic congestion caused by the large, cumbersome coaches.

They were held up several times, and Lucinda took the opportunity to study the fashionable ladies parading past under their parasols. Many wore dresses with pretty flounces at the hem, and Lucinda resolved to have her maid alter her own gowns in this mode.

The chaise swept them around Grosvenor Square and up to the verdant grassland of Hyde Park. Melanie suggested that they take a short stroll. As they walked under the glorious spreading oak trees, Melanie returned to the subject dearest to Lucinda's heart.

"Now," she declared, her soft brown eyes dancing with anticipation, "tell me what you and Miles have been up to!"

Nothing loath, Lucinda recounted her adventures.

When she had finished, Melanie gasped, "Lucinda, how incredible. How brave of you. To go alone at night to Medlow Grange. Then to journey to the Blue Boar and pose as a dancer. What daring! How I admire you!"

"It was your doing, in part," said Lucinda, "for it was you who lent me the book about Hannah Snell. Without that I would never have thought of running away to the Army with Miles. I realize now, of course, what an impossible scheme it was. But tell me . . . you have seen him?"

"He was waiting for me at the circulating library one day. He told me he was desperate to see you again, before he joined the Army. But before we could converse further, I suddenly felt faint. He kindly assisted me home, where he overheard my maid make a reference to my condition. It was then, of course, that we realized it would be the perfect excuse to bring you to London."

"I had guessed as much," sighed Lucinda. "Where and when are we to meet?"

"Tomorrow evening," replied Melanie, "at the Vauxhall Gardens."

Lucinda's pretty face clouded. "But what will Frederick say, when he sees me setting forth from the house alone, at night?"

"Frederick has a dinner engagement tomorrow night," said Melanie calmly. "And you will not be going alone. I shall accompany you."

"But you can hardly venture out at night in your condition!"

"Fudge!" laughed Melanie. "The child is not to be born until November, and I refuse to regard myself as an invalid for all the coming months. Besides, do you imagine I could possibly sit at home knowing you were out participating in an adventure? This time, I want to be there. I have always longed to visit Vauxhall, but Frederick has maintained it is a low place and refused to allow me to go."

"Then we shall most certainly go together tomorrow to meet Miles!" exclaimed Lucinda. "Oh, I can hardly wait!"

Melanie had arranged for them to journey by chaise to Westminster and then take the ferry down to Vauxhall. Lucinda was trembling with excitement as they glided in the boat along the Thames. The evening sun had turned the water to liquid gold and bathed the tall, riverside houses in a coppery glow.

On leaving the ferry at Vauxhall, the two girls entered the spacious gardens. How delightful, they agreed, were the cool avenues, bordered by shrubs and hedges of every conceivable variety. And as for the trees, they were like fantasies from fairyland, with their branches hung with lanterns and the lights glimmering through the leaves like a million stars.

Lucinda was enchanted, both by the gardens and the ladies and gentlemen who strolled along the avenues. All manner of people were gathered here, from the highest-born to the lowest, each and every one mingling with laughter and good humor. Ruffians, pimps, prostitutes, and the *ton* all rubbed shoulders, creating an atmosphere of dangerous glamor.

Lucinda could well imagine why Frederick had forbidden his wife to come here! The air of adventure and romance which cloaked Vauxhall would be sure to offend such a sober spirit as her brother Frederick.

"How are we to know where to find Miles?" Lucinda inquired, clutching Melanie's arm. "There are so many walks, and grottoes, we could so easily find ourselves lost."

"He advised me to follow the sound of the music," said Melanie serenely.

Sure enough, from beyond the arches ahead of them, they heard an orchestra playing. Guided by the melody, Lucinda and Melanie came to a music room, thronged with revellers listening to the orchestra and singers.

Lucinda would have paused and gazed on the decorated columns and the ornately painted ceiling. But almost before she had time to draw breath, she felt a touch on her arm. There, before her, executing his immaculate bow, was her masked gallant.

If Melanie had entertained any doubts about the depth of her sister's feelings towards Miles, they were immediately dispelled as she observed the radiance of Lucinda's face as she gazed upon him.

"So our plans succeeded," he said with a laugh. "Did I not promise you we would meet again, Lucinda?"

"You have never failed me," she smiled.

He seemed in lighthearted mood, and his gaiety was infectious. "Come, I have arranged a treat for us," he declared.

He escorted the two ladies out of the music room and down one of the avenues, until they reached a small rustic lodge set under the trees.

Inside, they found a most tempting cold supper laid out on a low table. There were cold meats of every description, mouth-watering strawberries and cherries, and wine.

"But how delightful!" exclaimed Melanie.

"Be seated," instructed Miles. "We shall have an excellent view of the fireworks from here."

It was one of the most memorable hours of Lucinda's life. In all her previous encounters with Miles, the situation had been fraught with danger. But here at Vauxhall they were able to relax and indulge in the simple luxury of enjoying one another's company.

Miles proved a most entertaining companion. And although the purpose of the occasion was to bring him and Lucinda together, he never for a moment made Melanie feel an outsider. As the fireworks splashed dramatic patterns across the sky, the three in the lodge feasted on strawberries and wine, and were merry.

When the fireworks were ended, Melanie arose. "I shall stroll back to the music room. Come and find me there later, Lucinda."

"But I cannot leave you on your own," Lucinda protested, darting to her feet.

Melanie smiled. "It is only a short step to the music room. I shall be quite safe, I promise you." She extended her hand to Miles. "Farewell, then, for the present. I wish you every good fortune."

He bent low over her hand. "I am ever in your debt, Lady Alford."

When Melanie had left them, Lucinda

posed the question which had puzzled her for a long time. "Miles, why do you always wear your mask? Surely here, in Vauxhall, you are unlikely to be recognized?"

He smiled. "It began as a jest, that night in March when I rescued you in the lane near your home. I couldn't resist slipping my neck-scarf over my face and masquerading as a highwayman! But over the following months, my mask has come to assume the nature of a serious symbol to me. I have vowed to wear it until my affairs in England are brought to a satisfactory honorable conclusion. It is a permanent reminder to myself that I must keep to my task. Until then, I regard myself as an outcast, and as such I wear my mask."

"I wish you would tell me more about yourself and your problems," said Lucinda. "I may be able to help. I would do anything—"

He took her hand. "I know, my sweet, dear Lucinda. But I am engaged in a deadly battle. And I must fight it alone. For your own safety, it is better that you know as little as possible about me." He shifted slightly on the seat and inquired, "Now tell me, did our plan succeed in delaying your marriage to Charles Somerford?"

Lucinda nodded. "My father agreed to postpone the wedding until Mr. Somerford is confirmed in his title. But Charles Somerford is a devious, cunning man. I am convinced he will think of some way to persuade my father that we should marry as soon as possible."

"You will never marry that man!" Miles's

voice curled like a whiplash. "I give you my word, Lucinda."

As always, his tone steadied and reassured her. She felt so safe with him, here in the lodge. But outside, it was growing dark, and she was aware that the time was rapidly approaching when she and Miles must part.

"You are going away to war," she said softly. "Will you not give me something to remember you by? Your neckscarf perhaps? Remember, you tied it around your face, in jest, that first time we met? It would be a memento for me during the long lonely days ahead when we are in different countries, separated by a wide stretch of sea."

Gently, he replied, "And how would you explain the matter, if your parents discovered that you had a gentleman's neckscarf hidden in your chamber?"

"I should pretend that it belonged to Robert," said Lucinda swiftly.

Miles shook his head. Lucinda guessed that he was reluctant to give her his neckscarf, for it must be embroidered with his monogram, and thus would give her a clue to his identity.

"I cannot give you the scarf," said Miles. "But you shall have a part of it."

As he spoke, he removed the black silk cloth from his neck. Deftly, he tore a thin strip from one side, and then said, "Give me a lock of your hair, Lucinda."

Surprised, she removed the little gold scissors from her etui case and snipped off a few of her golden hairs. He took the scissors from her and cut some of his own, blue-black hair. Holding the threads of black and gold he twisted them round the piece of silk, finally fashioning the cloth into a circle. Then, lifting Lucinda's right·hand, he slipped the ring onto her third finger.

"For the moment, it is all I have to offer you," he said softly. "I want you to keep it, as a symbol of my love for you."

Lucinda's eyes misted as she gazed down on her ring. How much it meant to her . . . the black silk, the raven hair and the gold, all entwined in a special message only she could understand.

"I shall keep it safe," she whispered. "I shall treasure it—oh, Miles!"

And then there were no more words, only his strong arms around her as he bent to cover her face in kisses.

They walked in silence back to the music room, where Miles escorted her across to Melanie before disappearing into the crowd. For a moment, surrounded by all the hubbub and laughter, Lucinda imagined she must have dreamed her meeting with Miles and their enchanting hour together in the lodge. But no, there was the reassuring pressure of his ring upon her finger to tell her that it had all happened. . . . he loved her . . . he would come back to her.

Lucinda smiled. And then, looking across to the window, she found she was gazing into the cold, pale blue eyes of Charles Somerford.

ELEVEN

Lucinda closed her eyes, frozen with horror. That evil man was here, in the music room of Vauxhall Gardens! Had he seen her with Miles? Was it possible that he had deliberately followed her all the way from Curzon Street?

Fearfully, she forced herself to open her eyes and look once more toward the window. He was gone. She cast around the music room, searching face after face, but there was no sight of him.

"Lucinda dear, is anything the matter? You look dreadfully pale."

Lucinda smiled wanly. "I thought . . . I imagined . . . no, I am perfectly well, Melanie. I expect I am simply suffering from the shock of saying farewell to Miles."

"Of course, how thoughtless of me," exclaimed Melanie. "Come, we shall go home directly."

Still there was no sign of Charles Somerford, and Lucinda was almost ready to believe that her fevered mind was deceiving her. As for the notion that he had followed her, why, that was clearly fanciful, for how could he know that she was in London?

And yet ... Lucinda could not shake from her mind the memory of those chilling blue eyes, boring into her across the crowded music room and claiming her for his own.

For the next few days, Melanie devoted herself to the task of distracting Lucinda from thoughts of Miles. They walked in St. James's Park and enjoyed delightful riverside drives along the Thames. Melanie introduced Lucinda to her friends, and there were tea parties, outings, and visits to the opera.

One morning, Frederick accompanied the ladies on a shopping expedition. Although not normally given to outward displays of emotion, even Frederick had been unable to quash a surge of pride at the realization that in November he would become a father. Accordingly, with Melanie and Lucinda in attendance, he could not resist, on that sunny June day, buying a splendid perambulator for his son.

"It is absolutely charming, Frederick," declared Melanie, as they gazed on the dark blue carriage, with its smart white shafts ready for the small pony which would draw the vehicle.

Frederick left instructions for his coat of arms to be painted on the side of the perambulator, and then the party strolled on until they reached the cabinetmakers. Lucinda was intrigued by the cabinetmaker's style of displaying his wares—neatly arranged outside his shop were perfect miniature models of the wardrobes, tables, and bookcases for sale inside.

Frederick, of course, had a ready explanation for this. "It is because of the small panes of glass in his window," he told Lucinda, "which would somewhat obscure our view of his wares if he displayed them as do other traders. Instead of causing us to squint through the glass, he makes small models of the items he has for sale and places them outside his establishment."

Melanie was not listening. She seized Lucinda's arm and pointed out a model of a shallow writing desk, with a high, elegantly carved back to it. "See, it is a screen writing table. Would it not be ideal for your Mama?"

Lucinda smiled. "Yes, it is just the thing! She is always complaining that if she brings her writing table near the fire, then her face becomes scorched, but if she sits away from the hearth, her poor feet freeze!"

"This solves her problem," declared Melanie. "See, her feet will keep warm, while the tall back of the table will screen her complexion from the heat of the fire. Frederick, may we order it for Lady Waverley?"

Frederick, in an amiable mood, was all agreement, and the three returned to Curzon Street well satisfied with their morning's purchases.

As they approached the house, however, their smiles turned to expressions of amazement. Blocking Curzon Street was a carriage bearing the Waverley coat of arms. Descending from it, looking extremely hot and bothered, was Lady Waverley herself.

Frederick hurried forward to assist her.

"Dear me, Mama looks thoroughly overwrought," murmured Melanie. "Now, Lucinda, kindly refrain from asking her any questions until she is seated in the drawing room and calmed and refreshed."

The next twenty minutes were agonizing for Lucinda. Whatever was her mother doing in London? How had her father come to allow it? Clearly, something was seriously amiss, but Melanie was wise in not allowing any queries until Lady Waverley had composed herself.

While the servants brought in the luggage and Melanie quietly gave instructions to her housekeeper about Lady Waverley's apartments, Lucinda and Frederick sat with their mother, listening to her account of the dreadful journey on badly rutted roads.

At last, Frederick, who was obviously as curious as Lucinda about his mother's unexpected arrival, leaned forward and said gently, "It is of course delightful to see you, madam. We are, unfortunately, a little unprepared—"

"I know," said Lady Waverley, still a little breathless, "but there was no time to advise you. In fact, there is so little time to arrange everything."

"Arrange what, madam?" pressed Frederick.

"Why, Lucinda's wedding, of course," declared Lady Waverley. "Her father has given his consent for her marriage to Charles Somerford to take place this coming Saturday!"

Lucinda gripped the arms of her chair, her face drained of color.

"You . . . you can't mean it, Mama," she whispered. She felt Melanie's cool hand on her shoulder and drew a measure of strength from her sister's reassuring presence.

Lady Waverley nodded. "Mr. Somerford came to visit your father two days ago. They were in the library for over an hour. It appears that the lawyers investigating his claim to the title of Duke of Lexburgh have given him an assurance that the whole matter will be resolved in the autumn. But, as Mr. Somerford pointed out, we will all be very much involved, then, making ready for the birth of our first grandchild. Mr. Somerford felt it would be too much of a burden for me, preparing for a birth and a wedding all at the same time. He was extremely concerned that the strain on me would be too great."

"How considerate of him," murmured Lucinda.

"So the upshot of it was, your father agreed that you should marry him at once, before the end of the London season."

Lucinda could hardly believe her ears. "You mean I am to be married in *London?* Papa is coming to the capital?"

"It seemed more convenient," said Lady Waverley. "After all, your father is due to make his annual visit here to sign all those boring financial papers with Frederick. Mr. Somerford will shortly be back in London. You are here visiting Melanie, and I have come to arrange your trousseau, so there seems little point in us all traipsing back to Waverley for the wedding."

A wave of despair swept over Lucinda. So Charles Somerford had outwitted her! Somehow, he must have heard that she was in the capital. He had followed her to Vauxhall and, yes, she was positive he had seen her with Miles!

Then how swiftly he had acted. He must have set forth immediately for Surrey and sought an interview with her father. Lucinda had no doubt that the story about the legal wrangles was a tissue of lies. Charles Somerford was clearly prepared to use any low means at his disposal to marry her and carry her off back to Derbyshire with all due speed.

Melanie inquired quietly, "Mama, where is Mr. Somerford now?"

"He has returned to his Derbyshire estates, to prepare his household for the arrival of his bride," smiled Lady Waverley.

Frederick frowned. "But surely, madam, you did not travel to London unescorted? I did not observe our steward, Hill, in the coach with you."

"No, Mr. Somerford very considerately lent me his own manservant, Dymoke, as escort. Would you be so kind as to quarter him here, Frederick, until the wedding on Saturday? Mr. Somerford felt Dymoke could be of great help to me, running errands and suchlike. There will be much to arrange, and Mr. Somerford said it would be unfair to impose upon your own servants and upset Melanie's domestic arrangements."

Melanie and Lucinda exchanged a swift glance. So Charles Somerford had effected yet another *fait accompli!* By installing his own manservant in Melanie's household, he had cleverly forestalled any attempt of Lucinda's to run away before the wedding. There was no doubt in either of the girls' minds that Dymoke was totally loyal to his master, and that he would have received instructions to keep the Lady Lucinda Verney under close watch every minute of the day until Saturday.

It was not until the following morning that the opportunity arose for Lucinda to have a confidential word with Melanie. In the green and gold morning room, as the sun streamed in through the windows, Lucinda gave vent to her despair.

"What am I to do, Melanie? Is there any way we may send word to Miles?"

Melanie shook her dark head. "I fear not, Lucinda. We have no notion where he lodges in London. And in any event, he will surely have departed for the war by now."

The two girls stared at one another, utterly dismayed. "I would help you if I could, Lucinda," whispered Melanie, "but I am completely at a loss to know what to do."

"I am trapped," murmured Lucinda. "Today is Tuesday. In four days' time I shall be married to Charles Somerford! And there seems to be no way in the world I can avoid it!"

Before Melanie could reply, Lady Waverley swept into the room.

"Come now, Lucinda, you know we have a busy day ahead of us. Run along and put on your bonnet."

As Lucinda left the morning room, Lady Waverley commented to Melanie, "Really, you would imagine a young girl would be delighted at the prospect of going out to choose her trousseau and be fitted for her wedding dress. But to look at Lucinda you would think she was going to her own execution!"

"Perhaps," hazarded Melanie, "she is having doubts about the marriage. After all, the arrangements have been made so swiftly."

Lady Waverley sighed. "Of course, all brides-to-be have fits of nerves. I did myself. It is only natural. I must endeavor to be more patient with Lucinda. I must show her more understanding."

Melanie tried again. "It does seem a pity, though, that she will be marrying a mere mister. I feel so guilty. If only my baby were not due in November, you would have the pride and pleasure of seeing your daughter receive her wedding ring and the title of Duchess."

"I only wish I had been present when Mr. Somerford saw Lord Waverley," confessed Lucinda's mother. "Of course the birth of your child and a wedding would not be too much for me to cope with. But I was out attending to a sick village girl when Mr. Somerford arrived, and I returned to the house to find the whole affair was settled."

Melanie looked thoughtful. Mr. Somerford must have been at his most persuasive that morning, she reflected. She felt intensely sorry for Lucinda, but although she wracked her brains all day for a solution, she could think of none. Despite all their efforts, Lucinda, it seemed, was doomed to marry a man she loathed.

As Saturday approached, Lucinda could not bring herself to express any interest in the preparations for her wedding. By Thursday, her mother had totally lost patience with her.

"Really, Lucinda, you must stop looking so uninterested," she protested, as they returned from yet another shopping expedition. "You would not stand still for a minute while the dressmaker was trying to fit your wedding dress. And when she showed you the samples of lace for your veil, why, you gazed out of the window and refused to make any choice at all! You put me quite to the blush!"

Lucinda glanced behind, at the solid, swarthy figure of Dymoke, who was walking behind carrying the parcels of silk lingerie that would comprise part of her trousseau. Wherever she and her mother had gone, Dymoke had accompanied them. Watchful, outwardly respectful, always obliging.

Lucinda hated Dymoke. Not for a moment had he allowed her out of his sight. When she left the house, he accompanied her. When she was inside the house, she often saw him strolling up and down Curzon Street, cutting off all means of escape.

She could sense the walls of fate closing in on her. She felt breathless, and slightly unreal, as if she were living in the midst of a nightmare. Her tortured mind was quite unable to accept that on Saturday, at eleven o'clock in the morning, she would become Mrs. Charles Somerford. She could not—would not—accept it.

Accordingly, she drifted like a person in a dream, taking no notice of what was happening around her. Saturday, she was convinced, would never come. It could not come. It *must* not!

But on Friday evening Lucinda was jerked harshly back into the world of reality by the arrival of her father at the house on Curzon Street. Lord Waverley was, of course, thoroughly out of temper and already complaining that the foul London air was sending him to an early grave. His teeth ached, his bones hurt, his dinner disagreed with him. In short, he could not wait for the wedding to be over, and his business finished, so he could return to his beloved Surrey.

After dinner, Frederick suggested that they pay a visit to his club, to discuss the family's financial business. The expedition caused a moment of light relief for Lucinda, as Lord Waverley announced his intention of travelling to the club in a sedan chair.

Even Frederick, traditionalist as he was, showed shock at this. "Sir, no one employs that mode of travel nowadays! Why, it is hopelessly out of style."

"A sedan is the right and proper way for a gentleman to travel when in town," insisted the Earl.

Trying to be helpful, Lady Waverley intervened, "Why not compromise, my lord?" she suggested. "Is there not one kind of sedan which is set on wheels instead of being carried along by two footmen?"

Lord Waverley snorted. "I never heard of anything so undignified! I refuse to be trundled along on wheels, like a load of compost on a gardener's barrow. Frederick, be so kind as to order your footman to call me a traditional sedan!"

Frederick, still muttering that he would be the laughingstock of all the club, had no choice but to comply.

Lucinda retired early that night, unable to face an evening of polite drawing room conversation with her mother. Her bedchamber overlooked the street, and there below, patrolling up and down, was the swarthy figure of Dymoke. Lucinda hastily drew across the silk curtain, unable to bear the sight of him.

"Oh, how different this was from all her girlhood dreams of the night before her wedding! As she stood poised on the threshold of a new life, these last few hours between girlhood and womanhood were such a special time.

Taking Miles's ring from her jewel case she reflected how joyful she would have felt had she been marrying him! With what excitement and anticipation would she have prepared herself, confident in the knowledge that in the morning she would become his wife. That tomorrow night he would come to her, and take her into his arms, and embrace her as a husband should.

Lucinda's hands flew to her face. But it would be the loathsome Charles Somerford who would come to her! It would be he to whom she would be compelled to submit. She would belong to him, body and soul. He could do with her as he willed, and no one in the whole world would have the power to stop him.

Her eyes filled with hot, angry tears. Then there came a tap on the door. Quickly, Lucinda dried her eyes as her mother came softly into the room. Lady Waverley seemed extremely ill at ease. She sat down in the chair by the window and fiddled with the fringe on her shawl.

"So, my daughter. Tomorrow you will be married. I felt it was only right, you know, that we should have a little talk before you go to the altar."

Despite her inner misery, Lucinda's sense of humor asserted itself. She was forced to bite her lip to prevent herself from laughing. She remembered her times with Miles, when he had held her in his arms and kissed her . . . the desire, the tumultuous passion they had shared.

Now, here was her mother, pink-cheeked, about to explain her duties as a wife. Lucinda knew she must stop her.

"Mama, it is very kind of you . . . but I believe I already know what you have come to tell me. Melanie and I have grown very close, you know, and—"

Lady Waverley sighed with relief. "Ah, yes. Dearest Melanie has no doubt been a great example to you as a dutiful wife." She stood up and took her daughter's hand. "Marriage is never easy, my dear. Just remember to be obedient and willing, and it will soften the way for you. I hope you will be happy."

Lucinda kissed her mother on the cheek. "Thank you, Mama." Happy? With Charles Somerford? Oh, how impossible!

Lucinda managed to contain herself until the door had closed behind her mother. Then, clutching Miles's ring, she flung herself down upon the bed and gave way to the tears she had held back for so long.

By ten o'clock on Saturday morning, Lucinda stood dressed in her wedding gown. She was alone in her chamber. Melanie and two maids had helped her to dress, lifting the delicate white silk gown over her head and pinning the filmy lace veil securely in place on her golden curls.

While her hair was being brushed, she had watched the hateful Dymoke depart for his master's lodgings in Grosvenor Street. Charles Somerford had planned to arrive back from Derbyshire last night, and now Dymoke had gone to prepare the bridegroom for his wedding. Charles Somerford had taken no chances, Lucinda thought wryly. He had ordered his manservant to remain at Curzon Street until the last possible moment, just in case his reluctant bride should attempt to escape.

But this time, thought Lucinda, there was no hope of any rescue. She gazed at herself in the mirror. She looked enchanting.

"But oh, Miles," she whispered, "this dress, this veil, this bride . . . all should have been for you."

In the dying moments of her girlhood, Lucinda relived her adventures with the man she loved. The rides through the night . . . the passionate embraces . . . the warmth of his lips on hers. Now it was over. She would never see him again. For once Charles Somerford's ring was upon her finger, she knew he would never allow her to wander at will. If Mr. Somerford was not there to guard her, then the sly Dymoke would be watching.

Lucinda settled the veil over her shoulders and reflected that at least she would have her memories of Miles. It was more than many girls had. They at least would give her comfort during the bleak years ahead.

At the door she paused and looked back on the room. It occurred to her then that she had slept alone for the last time. Tonight, and on all the other nights for the rest of her life, Charles Somerford, her husband, would have the right to enter her chamber and her bed.

Lucinda shuddered. Hastily, she closed the door behind her and walked down to the drawing room, where her family were assembled. Lady Waverley was dressed in gray silk, with Melanie beside her elegant in dark blue. The menfolk stood stiffly in formal black breeches and double-breasted tail coats.

Lord Waverley cleared his throat as he regarded Lucinda. "My word, you look lovely, my dear. Though why so sad? You should be radiant with joy on your wedding day."

"It is only natural that she should feel nervous," said Lady Waverley, coming across to adjust Lucinda's veil.

Frederick glanced at his watch. "I think we should be setting out for the church. The carriages are waiting."

Lord Waverley turned to his daughter. "Are you ready, Lucinda?"

"Yes, Papa." Her face was deathly pale.

"Lady Waverley, Melanie and I will travel in the first carriage," declared Frederick, "to arrive at the church shortly ahead of you and Lucinda, sir. The servants—"

Frederick broke off in surprise as the manservant Dymoke burst unceremoniously into the drawing room.

"My lord!" he gasped, his face flushed and perspiring.

"Compose yourself!" ordered Lord Waverley. "How dare you enter this drawing room unannounced, and in such a disorderley fashion? Can you not see that we are about to set forth for my daughter's wedding?"

"Yes, my lord," blurted Dymoke, "but that's what I hastened to tell you. My master, Mr. Somerford. He . . . well, he's gone!"

"Gone! What do you mean gone?"

"He is not at his lodgings, sir. There is no sign of him."

As Lord Waverley's face turned purple, Melanie quietly drew Lucinda into a chair. She found she was holding her breath, hardly daring to hope.

Frederick paced the room. "I imagine he has been delayed on the way back from his country estates. What a confounded nuisance!"

"Beggin' your pardon, sir," went on Dymoke, "but the arrangement was that Mr. Somerford would return to Grosvenor Street to collect some personal effects *before* he went up to Derbyshire. But I can see no sign of him having come to Grosvenor Street at all."

"Strange," mused Frederick. "Perhaps he decided to go straight to Derbyshire from Waverly and miss London altogether."

Lady Waverley subsided into the chair beside Lucinda. "We must discover where he is! It is too vexing of Mr. Somerford to be late, on his wedding day. I never heard of such a thing!"

"It is certainly unforgivably rude," murmured Melanie.

Frederick was all action. "The wedding will have to be postponed. I shall send my steward to the church to explain the delay. Meanwhile, Dymoke, you will ride posthaste to the Bush Inn at Finchley. If Somerford was riding north from either London or Surrey, he'd have been sure to stop there to change horses. They will know when he was last seen, and when—if—he is expected again."

Lord Waverley agreed to these plans, and Dymoke departed. Then Lord Waverley came across to Lucinda. "I am so very sorry, my dear," he murmured. "This must be a great disappointment to you."

Lucinda's heart was singing. "Yes, Papa," she whispered.

He patted her hand. "Take heart. There is bound to be a reasonable explanation for the delay." He scowled. "But damme, if there is *not*, then sure as death Mr. Somerford will have *me* to answer to!"

Melanie pressed a glass of wine into Lucinda's trembling hand. She sipped it gratefully. Could it be that, after all, Miles had not let her down? He had promised her faithfully that she should not marry Charles Somerford. *Trust me*, he had said. She knew not how, but in some mysterious fashion he had acted and once more come to her aid. She was convinced of it!

Even so, a chill struck her bones as she remembered Charles Somerford's evil, ruthless face. So Miles had managed to delay her wedding. But surely even he could not intervene forever?

Melanie took Lucinda upstairs, assisted her out of her wedding dress, and suggested she should rest. But that Lucinda could not do. Every moment she expected to hear a resounding knock on the door, heralding the arrival of the bridegroom . . . Charles Somerford, furious at the delay, but come to take her, willing or no, to the church to make her his wife.

TWELVE

The hours dragged past, but still the bridegroom did not appear. Sunday saw the return of Dymoke. He reported that the landlord of the Bush at Finchley had seen nothing of Mr. Somerford in the past month. He was not expected, and had sent no word that he would be arriving. Dymoke also informed Lord Waverley that the housekeeper at Grosvenor Street confirmed that her master had not returned there from Waverley.

Lord Waverley was beside himself with rage. "Dash it all, what is the counfounded fellow up to? How dare he treat my daughter in this cavalier fashion?"

"It is certainly most mysterious," murmured Lady Waverley.

"Mysterious? It is downright unforgivable! I give him permission—against my better judgment, I might add—to marry my daughter now instead of waiting until he's a duke, and what does he do? He disappears off into the blue!"

"Perhaps," ventured Lucinda, trying not to sound too cheerful, "he has met with an accident?"

"In which case he should have sent word," snapped Frederick.

"Well, my patience is exhausted," declared Lord Waverley. "I refuse to spend another day in this odious city. Frederick, is there any more business for me to attend to?"

"Nothing urgent, sir."

"In that case, kindly order my carriage. I am taking Lucinda and her mother back to the country immediately. And if that fellow should dare to show his face here—"

"Fear not, sir. I'll give him a sound horse-whipping!" Frederick promised grimly.

Two hours later, Lord and Lady Waverley were ready to depart. As Lucinda kissed Melanie goodbye, the dark-haired girl whispered, "If I hear anything of our friend, I will let you know."

Lucinda hugged her. "Oh, Melanie, I hardly dare hope. Farewell, and thank you!"

In the weeks that followed, all the fashionable ladies in the county called at Waverley Hall to express their sympathy for Lucinda. The jilted lady herself found it all highly diverting and adopted an air of forlorn bravery whilst inside her spirits were soaring.

"Dashed bad show," rasped Lady Falconbridge as she sat with Lady Waverley and Lucinda in the shade of an oak tree one hot August afternoon. "Still no word of the chap, I take it?"

"None," intoned Lucinda, attempting to sound mournful.

Lady Falconbridge cast her a shrewd glance. "Mmm. I always thought you'd be better off without him. The entire Somerford family are dissolute and unreliable."

Lady Waverley swatted a drowsy bee with her handkerchief. "But what has become of Mr. Somerford? How could he just disappear like that? No one seems to have the remotest notion where he could have gone."

Lady Falconbridge laughed. "Perhaps he ran off to join the Army. It seems to be the fashionable thing to do nowadays."

Lucinda started, wondering if by any strange chance, Lady Falconbridge could be referring to Miles.

"Just because Robert left to join the hussars, it does not mean that every other man of our acquaintance is going to do the same," said Lady Waverley tartly.

Nevertheless, Lady Falconbridge's chance remark was repeated in drawing rooms throughout Surrey and London. Gradually, it became accepted that Charles Somerford had gone to fight for his country. Of course, it was appalling of him to jilt poor Lucinda like that. But no doubt he felt the strong call of duty. As no one could think of any other explanation for his behavior, the idea of the Army seemed as reasonable as any.

September, however, brought news which drove speculation about Charles Somerford from everyone's head. Lord Waverley gathered his family together in the library and gravely informed them that his son Robert had been injured in the Rhinelands. He had been taken to a hospital some distance from the front, and although his condition was serious, he was expected to recover.

"But wounded in the chest!" wailed Lady Waverley. "And in a foreign hospital! Why, they don't even speak the same language! How is he to make himself understood? He will die, I know he will, alone in an alien land!"

It took Lucinda a full day to calm her mother and persuade her that Robert was blessed with a strong constitution.

"And after all," said Lucinda practically, "he is probably far safer lying resting in hospital than out in the front line fighting the French."

Although Lady Waverley saw the sense of her daughter's words, she remained restless. Lucinda was glad when Melanie arrived at the Hall to prepare for the birth of her child. Taken up with all the preparations in the nurseries, Lady Waverley's mind was diverted from the fate of her younger son.

Aware of the question that was uppermost in Lucinda's mind, Melanie hastened to assure her that she had received no word of or from Miles. Inevitably, the news of Robert's injury had increased Lucinda's fears for the man she loved, the man who was at this moment far away on foreign soil, with his life in danger every minute of the day and night.

One morning, the normal routine of the Hall was disrupted when Lord Waverley once more ordered his family into the library. Lady Waverley immediately called for her smelling bottle, convinced that her husband had received yet more bad intelligence about Robert.

As Lucinda entered the book-lined room she noticed that her father was holding a thick card, elegantly embossed in gold.

Clearing his throat, he declared, "I have to tell you all that we are summoned by the Prince Regent to a reception at Carlton House."

There was a moment of stunned silence. The only sound was that of the garden boy sweeping up the dead leaves outside.

"To Carlton House!" exclaimed Lady Waverley. "Oh, my dears, what an honor! Does it say, my lord, why we have been invited, what the occasion is, when—"

The Earl raised a hand. "No further information is given on the card, except that we are to present ourselves on the twenty-third of October, at seven o'clock."

"The twenty-third!" cried the Countess. "That is barely two weeks away. We have so little time to have new dresses made. To be sure, I have nothing suitable to wear to Carlton House!"

Lord Waverley frowned. "My dear, I fear

that although your name is included on the card, it will be impossible for you to accompany us. After all, Melanie can hardly attend the reception in her condition. And she cannot be left here alone."

Seeing her mother's acute disappointment, Lucinda said quickly, "I will stay with Melanie. Really, I have no interest in going to Carlton House."

Melanie would not allow this blatant untruth to pass. "Nonsense, Lucinda. Of course you shall go. And Lady Waverley, too. I am sure if I approach Lady Falconbridge, she will come and keep me company while you are away."

So it was arranged. The family set forth for Curzon Street on the morning of the twenty-second of October, thus giving them a full twenty-four hours in London to prepare for the Prince Regent's reception.

Carlton House! As they approached the great, impressive columns just before seven the following evening, it seemed as if the entire *haut monde* was thronging up the steps.

Lady Waverley was becoming agitated in her excitement. "Look, Lucinda, there is Lady Buckram. What magnificent sapphires! And see, there are Lord and Lady Cheshire. My, how grand they all look. I am sure they will think us rustic in comparison."

"Calm yourself, Mama," urged Frederick. "You and Lucinda both look charming."

Lucinda raised her eyebrows, for a compliment from her brother was a most unusual occurrence. But she did indeed look quite enchanting, in a gown of palest pink silk. Her golden hair was arranged in a cascade of fetching curls, while her slender throat was adorned with an amethyst necklace which matched exactly the rare color of her eyes.

They gathered with the rest of the guests in one of the great saloons of Carlton House. Never in her life had Lucinda seen such magnificence. She gazed up in wonder at the graceful columns which supported a silver cornice set against a lavender background. Above the columns, the beautiful sky-blue ceiling was hung with six shimmering chandeliers.

As the peers of the realm and their families formed two long lines in the saloon, Lucinda reflected that this was certainly *the* most dazzling occasion. Everyone was exquisitely dressed, and the saloon was soon filled with the glitter of priceless jewels, the rustle of silk, and the fragrance of expensive perfume.

Excitement mounted as the time approached for the Prince Regent himself to make his entrance. At last, the great double doors at the end of the saloon were flung open, and the Prince appeared with his retinue.

He was an impressive figure, formally attired in white breeches and a richly embroidered velvet dress coat. The Prince walked regally down the red carpet, smiling in acknowledgment of the bows and curtseys of the assembled company.

On reaching the dais at the end of the saloon, he turned and addressed his guests:

"I am most pleased to welcome you here

this evening," he said, in his firm, measured tones. "I have called you together to join me in honoring some of the fine, brave officers who have acquitted themselves so gloriously in our war against the French."

Lucinda saw that behind the Prince a footman had appeared, holding a blue velvet cushion on which were laid some medals.

"First," went on the Prince, "I ask you to pay tribute to an officer who has not only fought valiantly and with great courage on our behalf. He has also, and at great peril to himself, saved the life of a fellow officer. In so doing, he has the satisfaction of knowing that he has redeemed in full the honor of his family name. I call before you all the Duke of Lexburgh!"

The double doors were flung open. Lucinda felt the room spin around her. The Duke of Lexburgh! So it was true, then, that the loathsome Charles Somerford had indeed gone away to the war. And somehow, he had covered himself in glory and was to be received with honor and pomp by the Prince Regent himself!

Lucinda felt Frederick's hand on her arm, steadying her. Taking a deep breath, she raised her head, prepared to look Charles Somerford boldly in the face as he advanced toward the Prince. Dazed, she watched the immaculately dressed officer striding past the lords and ladies, down the red carpet toward her.

It seemed to Lucinda that her memory must be playing her false. Surely Charles Somerford had never been that tall, that imposing? She blinked, to clear her vision.

A flutter of hope stirred within her. No, she had not been mistaken! That man was not Charles Somerford. It could not be! But who?

And then her heart missed a beat. She knew that manly stride, the commanding set of those shoulders! Yet how could it be? What trick of fate . . . ?

He was nearly upon her. Lucinda could hardly breathe for the joy that consumed her. For it was not Charles Somerford's evil face into which she gazed, but that of the man she loved, her beloved Miles!

His mask had gone, revealing his strong, handsome features. As he drew level with her, in that single split second, he caught her eye. And she was sure he winked at her!

Lady Waverley turned to her husband and hissed, "What is this, my lord? That man cannot be the Duke of Lexburgh! The title was due to pass to Mr. Somerford! That officer must be an impostor. You must denounce him as such to the Prince forthwith!"

Too late. Already, Miles was kneeling before the Prince Regent and the gold medal was being pinned to his chest, amidst resounding applause from all the distinguished guests.

Lucinda's heart surged with pride. Never had she experienced such a fever of excitement and impatience. Oh, how she longed to rush and fling herself into Miles's arms. There were a million questions she wanted to ask—but they could wait. For the moment, all she desired was to hear his voice once more. To gaze into his gray eyes. To know that she belonged to him, and that he would never leave her again.

But the ceremony was by no means over. There were other war heroes to be honored. Lucinda had to curb her impatience and watch Miles take his place behind the Prince and wait whilst a line of other, lesser officers entered the saloon to receive their medals.

At last, the formal part of the evening was over, and the Prince gave the signal for the orchestra to play. Lucinda could not take her eyes from Miles. She saw him speak to one of the Prince's aides ... who then led the tall, dark officer across to the silk-draped window where she stood with her family.

As he approached, Lucinda dared not look at him, lest her mother should happen to glance at her and see in her eyes all the love shining forth for the Duke.

The aide was addressing her father. "Lord Waverley, the Duke of Lexburgh has requested the honor of being introduced to you and your distinguished family. I also feel constrained to tell you what the Duke will not—namely, that it was your son whose life he saved in the Rhinelands."

Lucinda kept her eyes firmly on the carpeted floor, whilst her father exclaimed, proffered his thanks, his gratitude . . . and the Duke demurred, insisting that he had merely acted as any soldier should in defense of a fellow officer.

Lucinda could guess what had happened. Had not the Prince himself declared that Miles had saved Robert's life at great peril to himself? Clearly, the hot-headed Robert had recklessly hurled himself into the line of fire. Miles had galloped to the rescue, laying himself open to attack as he did so.

Then she heard her father say, "May I present Lady Waverley, my son and heir, Viscount Alford, and my daughter Lucinda."

The moment had come. Lucinda dipped a curtsey, then lifted her lovely head as Miles bent low over her hand. Oh, how handsome he looked, with the Prince's medal gleaming proudly on his dark green velvet dress coat He held Lucinda's hand just a fraction longer than was necessary and flashed her a brief, laughing glance.

Then, turning to her father, he said gravely, "I am delighted to make your acquaintance, my lord. Though I suspect you are surprised to find me bearing the title of Duke of Lexburgh."

Lady Waverley had the grace to blush. Only twenty minutes before, she had been ready to denounce him as an impostor! But Lucinda could see that her mother was truly overwhelmed with Miles's dignified bearing, his rugged good looks and impeccable manners.

The Earl said, "We were indeed under the impression that one Charles Somerford was the heir to the late Duke of Lexburgh."

Miles nodded. "When the young Duke was found so tragically drowned, the situation was somewhat involved. As you may know, the old Duke of Lexburgh had two brothers. The younger, now dead, was Charles Somerford's father."

"We had heard as much," said Frederick. "The elder brother had disappeared to Europe and could not be traced."

"That brother was Darcy, my father," explained Miles. "He was a good man, but possessed of a restless spirit."

As are you, thought Lucinda, smiling to herself.

"He wandered to Italy," Miles went on, "and married an extremely beautiful countess, who was only too happy to drift around Europe with my father. I was their only child."

"So you had an extremely unsettled childhood?" inquired Lady Waverley sympathetically.

The Duke smiled. "We had no permanent home, it is true. But in many ways I enjoyed a far more interesting education than a formal kind of tuition would have offered me. However, my mother, though adorable, was extremely extravagant. When she and my father died, of a fever in Spain, there was very little left of our share of the family fortune."

"Meanwhile, in England, the old Duke and his son had been steadily squandering their portion of the Somerford wealth," muttered Lord Waverley.

Miles looked him full in the eyes. "It was for this reason that I joined the Army. It seemed to me the only way in which I could in some measure redeem my family name."

"That you have done in full, sir," commented Frederick.

Lord Waverley frowned. "But why did you not claim your title months ago? Surely you must have been aware that after the young Duke was found drowned, your cousin Charles was claiming the title?"

"I knew nothing of the tragedy until I returned to England following my own parents' death," replied the Duke. "I was shocked to learn of the drowning incident, and even more appalled to discover to what depths our family name had sunk. As a matter of principle I felt I could not claim the title until I had proved *myself* worthy. For I knew that by so doing, I would once more bring honor to the name of Somerford."

Lucinda sensed that Miles was anxious to avoid any more questions on the subject, especially those concerning his cousin Charles. Fortunately, before Lord Waverley could say another word, supper was announced.

"Lord Waverley," smiled Miles, "may I have your permission to escort your charming daughter in to supper?"

Lady Waverley looked delighted. That the acclaimed war hero, the dashing Duke of Lexburgh—the gallant officer who had rescued her son Robert—should be seen by the *haut monde* escorting her own Lucinda at the Prince Regent's reception! There was glory indeed!

Lord Waverley gladly gave his consent. And the eyes of every fashionable lady in the saloon were fixed jealously on Lucinda as the Duke of Lexburg led her into the supper room.

Each table was decked with delicious delicacies of every description, but Lucinda was

233

too overcome to feel hungry. Miles drew her into a secluded arbor. For a long moment, they were content just to sit and gaze on one another, and delight in being together once more.

"Miles, I can hardly believe it is all true!" Lucinda murmured. "When the doors opened and you strode into the saloon! It is a wonder I did not faint right into your arms!"

He laughed. "I am sorry to have shocked you so. But it would not have been right, before, to have told you who I was."

"But what about Charles Somerford? Where is he? Do you know, I was about to set out for my wedding—things had gone that far —but he did not appear."

Miles's face darkened. "What I am about to tell you is for your ears only, Lucinda. Enough mud has been cast on my family name. I will not add to it by making public the truth about Charles Somerford. What happened is this: I came to England intending to make myself known to my cousin, the new Duke of Lexburgh. I was amazed to learn that he had drowned."

"It was very tragic," sighed Lucinda.

"It was very peculiar," said Miles grimly, "for all my family are extremely strong swimmers. The Somerfords are noted for their prowess in the water, and I had heard that my cousin could outstroke us all."

"The story was that the young Duke had been drinking heavily," said Lucinda. "He must have toppled into the water and then fainted."

"My suspicions were aroused," said Miles,

234

"and I decided to investigate. No one in Derbyshire knew my identity, so I asked some questions of the servants on the estate. I discovered that my cousin had indeed been drinking that day . . . with Charles Somerford."

Lucinda's eyes widened. "What was so strange," went on Miles, "was that Charles Somerford and the young Duke up until that time had hardly been on speaking terms. The servants told me that my cousin the Duke regarded Charles Somerford as an arrogant boaster. He would have no truck with him."

Lucinda's opinion of the late Duke began to rise.

"Then," said Miles, "when I heard that Charles Somerford was already claiming the title for himself, I determined to keep him under close watch until I had got to the bottom of the matter. Of course, he had no idea that I even existed. Nothing had been heard of my father for years. He must have decided that if he could remove the young Duke, there would be nothing to stop him from inheriting the title."

"But how could you prove that there was foul play involved in the young Duke's death?" asked Lucinda.

"That took some time, and a considerable amount of money," Miles told her. "I knew I had time on my side, for as my parents had moved around so much it would take Charles Somerford's lawyers many months to track them to Spain, and ascertain that they were indeed dead. Meanwhile, I employed some agents of my own to question further the servants at the Derbyshire estate, whilst I kept an eye on Charles himself in Surrey."

"And what did you discover?" breathed Lucinda.

"On the evening the young Duke was drowned," said Miles, "one of the village girls was washing her clothes in the river. She saw Charles Somerford and the Duke stroll down the path. There was an argument. Charles Somerford hit the Duke, who fell into the river. He began to swim toward the bank, but Somerford seized him and held him under the water until he was dead."

"Miles!"

"The servant girl was terrified. She tried to hide, but sharp-eyed Somerford noticed her. He beat her unmercifully, threatening to kill the poor girl if ever she revealed what she had seen. Naturally, she kept silent for a long time. But when my agents began asking questions, she was so frightened she ran away. Naturally, this aroused my men's suspicions, and they brought her to me in London. I promised her my protection, and she told me all. I hope she will shortly be safely employed in your sister Melanie's household."

"And Charles Somerford?" inquired Lucinda. "Where is he? Why did he disappear?"

"As soon as I had the girl's testimony," said Miles, his voice icy, "I laid in wait for Somerford. I knew he was returning to London from Waverley, on his way back to his Derbyshire estate. I waylaid him by night on Vauxhall Bridge. I won't go into details of the scene, but we had an extremely ugly fight. Once the fellow realized that I knew the truth, he was determined to kill me."

Lucinda's throat tightened as she imagined the scene beneath the yellow lights of Vauxhall Bridge.

"He drew a pistol on me. But after a violent struggle, I managed to smash it with my swordstick. The pistol went off, firing into the villain's chest. He staggered backwards, and plunged over the bridge, into the swirling waters below."

"His ... body has not been found," whispered Lucinda.

Miles shook his head. "The currents in that part of the Thames are strong. By now, he will have been washed downriver and into the sea."

"It was a form of justice, then," mused Lucinda, "for after drowning the young Duke, Charles Somerford, too, went to a watery grave. But why did you not publicly denounce him, and tell the world what had happened? As it is, everyone believes the rumor that he went off to war, to fight gallantly for his country."

"Let them continue to believe that," declared Miles. "As I said, there has been enough disgrace and scandal attached to my family. And it has ended well. I am now the rightful Duke of Lexburgh. At the first opportunity, my dearest Lucinda, I intend to ask your father for your hand in marriage."

As he spoke, he raised her hand and kissed it. Lucinda gazed at him with shining eyes. "Miles, I can hardly believe that we are really to be married. When I think of all that has happened . . . all our secret meetings . . ."

"Ah, yes," he smiled, "there is one thing left to be done. Before we are wed, I shall put on my mask for the last time and journey to Medlow Grange, to replace the gold in Ellen Fitzjohn's summer house. I feel it is only right. And who knows, at some time in the future perhaps it may provide an adventure for another pair of lovers."

"You are an incurable romantic!" laughed Lucinda. "But I wish to come with you to replace the gold."

"You shall do no such thing," he protested. "Why, in a short space of time you will become the Duchess of Lexburgh, a respected, respectable matron. It would be most unseemly for you to ride through the moonlit countryside with a masked man!"

Lucinda's eyes twinkled. "I have to advise you, my lord, that I shall never be a respectable matron, as you well know."

"No," laughed Miles, "there is too much of the free, wild spirit in you for that. It is what I love about you, Lucinda."

"Then I shall ride wth you to Medlow Grange," she declared firmly.

On a crisp autumn night, when the sky was full of stars, Lucinda and Miles rode side by side to return the gold to Ellen's summer house. Miles laid the bag of gold back into the hollow of earth, and Lucinda carefully replaced the yellow tile.

"Thank you, Ellen," she murmured.

Holding aloft her candle, she glanced around the summer house. "You know, Miles, I sense a different atmosphere here now. That air of tragedy and longing has been swept away. Do you think poor Ellen has been watching over us . . . and because we have fallen in love, she, too, has found the peace for which she was so desperately searching?"

Miles bent and gently touched her face. "I am convinced of it, my lovely one."

As Miles lifted her out through the window of the ivy-covered ruin, Lucinda whispered, "How much has happened since we were last here. Then I felt chilled with sadness, knowing you were going away to the war. I was terrified I would never see you again."

He took her into his arms. "This *is* the last time," he breathed, "that we shall adventure together as the masked stranger and the rebellious golden-haired lady . . ."

And in the moonlight, he crushed her to him, his mouth warm and demanding. Willingly she surrendered to his passion, finding in his kisses and the masculine strength of his embrace a joy and rapture far beyond her wildest imaginings.

When at last the tide of ecstasy subsided, she was still for a moment within the circle of his arms. Then she reached up and removed the black silk mask from his handsome face.

"I love you," he declared. "With all my heart and soul I love you—my future Duchess."

She replied with starlight in her eyes: "And I love you, my lord Duke."

He drew her once more to him and kissed her for a long, long time. Then he said, "Come, my precious Lucinda. Our future together awaits us."

They were married just before Christmas, with Melanie as matron of honor. Robert, fully recovered from his injury, returned in time for the wedding.

The only member of the Verney family not present was the youngest, Lord Waverley's grandson, who was safely tucked up in his crib. Melanie had been adamant that they must name the baby Miles, and the entire family had approved her choice.

The new Duchess of Lexburgh was taken by her husband to his family seat in Derbyshire. As she anticipated, he proved to be a considerate husband and a passionate lover. He gave her everything her heart desired, and she was sublimely happy.

On her toilet table stood silver boxes crammed with priceless necklaces, bracelets, and rings. But one special piece she kept separate from all the rest, in its own velvet-lined case. It was a simple circle of black silk, entwined with raven hair and with gold.

And above the diamonds, sapphires, emeralds, and rubies, this was the jewel Lucinda treasured most of all.